Chapter 1

The October air carried the scent of decaying leaves and the distant, sweet smoke of autumn fires. Laney and Hekate sat across from me on the weathered picnic table, their faces scrunched in concentration. Each year, the amateur pumpkin carving contest beckoned with its promise of laughter and community cheer, but this year the stakes had soared with the television crews and that hefty prize.

Hekate wielded her knife with a precision that belied her age, her little hands dancing around the pumpkin's thick skin. "I'm thinking a traditional approach," she mused, her voice a shade darker than one might expect from a child so young. "A tribute to the origins of Samhain."

Laney's eyes sparkled with ambition. "I'm going big. A whole witch's scene—cauldron, broomsticks, the works."

I chuckled as I scooped out handfuls of seeds and pulp. "Careful not to carve too much ambition into that pumpkin, or it'll upstage us all."

Meri perched atop the fence, his black coat melding with the shadows as dusk crept closer. "You could use a bit more finesse, Kinsley," he drawled, his eyes glinting with mischief.

I raised an eyebrow at him. "Why don't you try? Your claws are sharper than any knife."

He yawned, displaying an impressive set of fangs. "And ruin my perfect paws? I think not."

Bonkers had been prowling around our feet, tail high in excitement. In one swift motion, he pounced on an unattended pumpkin, his considerable weight proving too much for the orange canvas. The gourd split open with a wet pop, sending seeds flying.

Laughter bubbled up from all three of us as Bonkers sat in the midst of his carnage, looking utterly pleased with himself.

Laney scooped up a seed and flicked it at him. "That's one way to make a jack-o'-lantern!"

Hekate giggled, plucking seeds from her hair. "Maybe we should enter that in the 'abstract' category."

I stood to gather paper towels for cleanup when Thorn's truck rumbled into the driveway. He stepped out with his usual measured grace, his sheriff's badge catching the last rays of sunlight.

"Looks like I missed quite the party," he said, a smile tugging at his lips as he surveyed our messy tableau.

"Bonkers decided to show off his carving skills," Laney explained while Hekate waved him over to inspect her near-complete masterpiece.

Thorn leaned down to kiss my cheek before crouching beside Hekate. "That's quite impressive," he praised before turning to Laney's ambitious project and whistling softly.

"Why are you home so soon?" I arched an eyebrow at Thorn, my hands still occupied with the wet paper towel I had grabbed for cleanup.

Thorn feigned a wounded expression, the corners of his eyes crinkling with barely concealed humor. "What, I'm not welcome here? Should I just turn around and head back to the station?"

I couldn't help but laugh, tossing the damp towel in his direction with playful precision. It hit his shoulder with a satisfying smack. "You know that's not what I meant."

He caught the towel mid-flight, a mock scowl on his face. "Just had the chance to clock out early, so I took it." His smile returned as he watched Bonkers now attempting to fit into the hollowed-out remains of his pumpkin conquest.

I paused, considering his words. Lately, Thorn had been making it a point to arrive home right on time, a change from his unpredictable schedule in the past. I knew the underlying reason for this newfound punctuality; he was concerned that Lisa might make another move against me. Despite my assurances that I could handle Lisa myself, he insisted on being there to protect me.

"You know," I began, brushing pumpkin residue from my hands onto my apron, "I've told you before, I can handle Lisa."

He nodded slowly, his eyes meeting mine with that steadfast gaze that always managed to reassure me despite my own protests. "I know you can. But it doesn't hurt to have backup."

The laughter and chaos of our impromptu pumpkin massacre still echoed in the yard as Thorn folded his arms, a gentle reminder sparkling in his eyes. "Don't forget, tonight we kick off the festival. It's the first of three nights, and I hear the competition's fierce this year."

I leaned against the picnic table, wiping a stray strand of curly red hair from my face with the back of my hand. "I haven't forgotten. How could I with Laney and Katie buzzing about it all week?" I glanced at my daughters, their faces alight with excitement for the night ahead.

Thorn's gaze followed mine, softening as he watched them. "They've been looking forward to this almost as much as Christmas." He chuckled. "Laney has her heart set on that giant teddy bear prize, and Katie... well, she just wants to show off her carving skills."

I smiled at the thought of Hekate standing proudly beside her pumpkin creation, already imagining her dark eyes shining with pride under the festival lights. "She's got talent, that one. Might just give those professionals a run for their money someday."

Thorn nodded in agreement before reaching out to brush a smear of pumpkin from my cheek. His touch was gentle, warm—comforting in a way that went beyond the simple act of affection. "We should get ready soon. The opening ceremony starts just after sunset, and I wouldn't want to miss it."

"Neither would I." I pushed off from the table and stretched, feeling the pull of anticipation for the night ahead. The festival had always been a highlight in Coventry, a time when magic felt closer to the surface, thrumming in the air alongside the scent of cinnamon and roasted nuts.

As I watched Laney and Hekate with their pumpkins—Laney's face alight with creative fire and Hekate's etched with an almost otherworldly focus—I couldn't help but feel a swell of pride. These moments were precious; they were what life was truly about.

"All right," I said, "let's clean up this mess and transform ourselves from pumpkin slayers to festivalgoers." The words had barely left my lips before Meri leapt from his perch on the fence with a graceful bound.

"And maybe find Bonkers a pumpkin he can't destroy," Meri quipped dryly as he sauntered past us, tail high.

Thorn laughed, his eyes crinkling at the corners in that way that always made my heart skip just slightly faster. "Let's make it a night to remember."

* * *

The night air, crisp and scented with autumn's harvest, wrapped around us as we approached the festival grounds. The girls cradled their pumpkins with a protective gentleness that belied the eerie faces they had carved into them. I carried my own creation, a whimsical design featuring a witch flying across a moonlit sky – an homage to the craft, sans actual witchcraft. We'd agreed, no magic in the carving; it wouldn't be fair to the other competitors.

The hubbub of the festival swirled around us – laughter, music, and the murmur of excited voices discussing the televised event. Thorn had his hands free, ready to assist if any of our pumpkin masterpieces showed signs of toppling.

"Remember, girls, this is just for fun," I reminded them as we joined the line to enter our pumpkins.

Laney nodded solemnly. "I know, Mom. But I still want to win."

Hekate chimed in with a grin that showed off her missing front teeth. "Me too! And my pumpkin is the spookiest!"

I couldn't help but chuckle at their competitive spirit. And I couldn't lie to myself… I said "it's just for fun" to the girls because that's what a good mom would do, but I wanted to win.

While we waited to fill out our entry forms, my attention was drawn to a couple of people locked in a heated exchange just beyond the sign-up table. Their words were muffled by the festival's din, but their body language spoke volumes – tight jaws, pointed fingers, and stiff postures.

"Thorn," I whispered, nodding subtly toward them. "Do you recognize those two?"

He followed my gaze and his brow furrowed in recognition. "That's Jacob Appleton," he said after a moment. "And I think the woman might be Essie Elrod."

My curiosity piqued. "Jacob Appleton and Essie Elrod? The pumpkin carvers? The pro pumpkin carvers?"

"Yeah," he confirmed with a slight nod. "There's been some tension between them for a while now."

"What kind of tension?" I pressed on.

Thorn shook his head slightly. "Nothing that's reached my department officially. Rumors mostly – accusations of stolen ideas and bad blood over competitions. Shouting matches that get annoying, but nothing that gets physical or really threatening."

The argument seemed to reach its peak; Jacob threw his hands up in exasperation before storming off into the crowd. Essie stood there for a moment longer, fists clenched at her sides before she too disappeared from view.

The line moved forward and I focused back on my family. "Well, let's hope tonight's about carving pumpkins and not rehashing old disputes."

Laney tugged on my sleeve, holding up her form with pride. "Mommy, look! I filled it out all by myself."

I took the paper from her and checked it over with an approving smile. "Perfect job, Laney." Then I ruffled Hekate's hair affectionately as she showed me hers.

Thorn leaned closer and murmured with a wry smile that softened his rugged features, "Let's make sure these pumpkins get all the attention they deserve."

I could feel the buzz of excitement radiating from Laney and Hekate as we made our way through the festival. The promise of victory danced in their eyes, each one certain they'd outdone the other with their carved creations. "I'm going to win," Laney declared with the confidence only a nine-year-old could muster.

Hekate, a couple of years her junior but not lacking in spirit, piped up in response, "No way, Laney. My pumpkin is way scarier!"

I smiled at their banter. The thought of winning flickered through my own mind, but I kept it to myself. After all, it was supposed to be about family fun – not competitive glory. "Girls, you're both winners as far as Daddy and I are concerned."

As we wandered amongst the stalls and displays, everything seemed dipped in shades of orange and infused with pumpkin spice. There were lattes steaming in cups clutched by cold hands, cocoa topped with whipped cream and a dusting of cinnamon, and fried pumpkin cheesecake that threatened to tip the scales of indulgence. It was a veritable pumpkin paradise.

Thorn wrinkled his nose as we passed yet another stand advertising pumpkin-spiced something-or-other. "Isn't this a bit much?" he asked, eyeing a sign for pumpkin spice popcorn.

I chuckled, linking my arm through his. "It's fall –
pumpkins reign supreme." I teased him with a nudge.
"But don't worry; I'm sure there's some apple cider
around here somewhere."

Hekate tugged at my sleeve with an eager glint in her
eyes. "Mommy, can we try the pumpkin spice fried
cheesecake? Please?"

Laney bounced on her toes beside her sister, nodding
vigorously. "And the cocoa! We have to try the cocoa!
I want mine with extra cinnamon!"

Their enthusiasm was infectious and even Thorn
couldn't resist their pleading faces. I caught his smile
as he looked down at them. "All right," he relented.
"But just one treat each."

"One?" Laney's eyes went wide as she surveyed the
array of options.

"Just one for now," I clarified with a wink that
promised more treats later.

We agreed on sampling a bit of everything – sharing
bites so we could savor all the festival had to offer
without overdoing it too early in the evening. With
each new taste – spicy sweetness melting into warmth
– I couldn't help but revel in these moments together
as a family.

Even Thorn found something to enjoy when we stumbled upon a stall selling fresh baked apple cider muffins slathered with cinnamon sugar butter. The aroma alone was enough to draw him in, and after one bite, he was hooked.

"I suppose this makes up for all the pumpkin," he said between mouthfuls, a contented sigh escaping him.

Laney giggled as she licked pumpkin spice frosting from her fingers, while Hekate savored her sip of cocoa, dark eyes shining above the rim of her cup.

It might have been pumpkiny overkill for some, but for us? It was just right.

I lingered at the edge of the display, marveling at the pictures of pumpkins transformed into works of art. They were a far cry from the toothy grins and triangle eyes that most associate with jack-o'-lanterns. These were sculptures, the raw orange flesh chiseled into delicate filigree, mythical creatures, and haunting visages that seemed to peer into your soul.

"Look at this one, Mommy," Laney said, pointing to a photo of a pumpkin with an entire forest scene carved into its surface. Tiny animals peeked from behind intricately rendered trees, and you could almost hear the whisper of leaves in a phantom breeze.

"It's beautiful," I admitted, leaning in for a closer look. The detail was astonishing—every leaf vein was etched with precision, every creature's fur looked soft enough to touch.

Hekate pulled at my hand, her eyes wide with excitement as she guided me to another picture. "This one's got dragons!" she exclaimed. Indeed, the pumpkin in the photo was adorned with dragons mid-flight, their scales and wings crafted so realistically it felt like they could burst from the gourd at any moment.

I overheard snippets of conversation from onlookers gathered around the display. Jacob's name came up time and again, accompanied by nods of respect and whispers of awe. "He's a shoo-in for the prize," one man said confidently to his companion. "No one can touch Appleton when it comes to pumpkins."

It wasn't just local pride boosting Jacob's reputation; there was genuine admiration for his skill. Despite this being Coventry's local event, word had spread beyond our town's borders. Carvers from other states had come seeking glory and the hefty prize money that now sweetened the pot.

The competition was fierce this year; it had to be with stakes like these. The chatter around me confirmed what I already suspected—Jacob Appleton was a force in the world of pumpkin carving. And yet, seeing these pictures brought home just how much talent and passion went into this craft.

Thorn squeezed my shoulder gently as he joined us in front of another awe-inspiring display photo—a pumpkin transformed into an entire underwater scene complete with coral, fish, and even a mermaid whose hair seemed to flow with unseen currents.

"Can you believe these are just pumpkins?" I murmured to him.

He shook his head in amazement. "They're incredible." His voice carried that note of respect he reserved for things that truly impressed him.

"Mommy," Laney asked after a moment of quiet contemplation, "do you think you could make something like this?"

I smiled down at her earnest face. "Maybe not exactly like this," I said honestly. "These carvers are artists with their own styles and years of practice."

"But you're really good too," Hekate piped up with fierce loyalty.

I ruffled her hair affectionately. "Thank you, sweetie." I glanced back at the photos before us.

As we moved away from the display to continue enjoying the festival's offerings, I couldn't help but feel a flicker of creative inspiration mixed with admiration for my fellow carvers—especially Jacob Appleton, whose skill had set a high bar for tonight's competition.

Chapter 2

As the autumn evening air grew crisp and the last glimmers of sunlight vanished behind the horizon, the crowd huddled together in eager anticipation. Pumpkin spice and excitement mingled in the air, as families and enthusiasts alike pressed closer to the stage where the professional pumpkin carvers were set to be introduced.

Ted Mellon, with his camera-ready smile and an enthusiastic wave, stepped onto the stage, microphone in hand. The buzz in the crowd heightened as he began to speak, his voice a warm baritone that filled the night.

"Ladies and gentlemen, boys and girls," Ted announced, "welcome to the grand introduction of this year's master carvers!"

A cheer erupted from the audience as each carver was called forward. One by one, they stepped up, their faces lit by a mix of pride and competitive fire. However, a ripple of confusion swept through the crowd as Ted arrived at a particular name on his list.

"And now," he continued, his eyes briefly flickering with uncertainty before he caught himself, "let's hear it for Jacob Appleton!"

Silence fell. No one moved toward the stage. Whispers wove through the spectators like wind through cornstalks.

Ted cleared his throat. "Well, it seems Jacob hasn't joined us just yet." He offered a lopsided grin that didn't quite reach his eyes. "But let's continue with our talented lineup!"

I scanned the faces of the carvers for reactions. That's when I caught sight of Essie Elrod standing off to one side. Her lips curled into a smile not quite suited for a missing colleague—more like she had just heard her favorite song come on.

The introductions carried on, but Ted's stumble over Jacob's absence hung over us like an ominous cloud threatening rain. Carvers spoke briefly about their passion for pumpkin artistry, each one adding to the festive atmosphere but none erasing the question mark that Jacob's empty spot created.

Finally, Ted wrapped up with a few more words about HappyTummy Organic Farms and their generous sponsorship before stepping down from the stage. The crowd dispersed slowly, clusters forming as people speculated about Jacob's whereabouts.

"Think he got cold feet?" Thorn murmured beside me as we navigated away from the throng.

I shook my head. "Jacob? No way. He lives for this competition."

Thorn nodded, looking out across the sea of carved pumpkins that glowed under the night sky like amber jewels.

Essie was still visible in the dimming light, her face alight with a triumph that seemed out of place amidst concern for Jacob's absence.

I couldn't shake off a nagging feeling—a premonition that there was something more behind her smile and Jacob's missing presence than mere rivalry or schadenfreude.

I found myself lingering near the photo display, my gaze tracing the intricate lines of Jacob's carvings in the captured images. They were truly mesmerizing, each one evidence of a craft perfected over years of dedication. Beside me, Clara Greenway stood still as a statue, her eyes fixed on the same photos with an intensity that seemed to transcend mere appreciation.

"Remarkable, isn't it?" I ventured, hoping to draw her out.

Clara started slightly, then composed herself. "Yes," she said, her voice a quiet murmur. "Jacob always sets the bar high." But there was a tightness around her eyes, a hard set to her jaw that spoke of something deeper than respect.

I watched her intently, letting the quiet linger before I hesitantly redirected my focus, instantly met with the whirlwind of gossip permeating the throng. Jacob Appleton's nonappearance acted as a void, drawing in various speculations. A number of aficionados surmised he might be hidden away, applying final strokes to a work that would astonish his rivals, while subdued murmurs suggested something more sensational—a swift and unexpected retreat from the tournament he had reigned over for years. Maybe he had finally lost his touch… or his will to compete…

Thorn sidled up beside me, his eyes following Clara as she moved away from the display with reluctant steps. "You see that?" he asked softly.

"The way she looks at his work?" I replied. "Hard to miss."

He nodded and leaned in closer. "Jacob's not just competing against time and pumpkin flesh," he explained. "There's a history there with Jonas Thompson—his neighbor."

"Competition is healthy," I mused aloud, "but some of this seems personal."

"It's more than just rivalry," Thorn confirmed. "Jonas has been in Jacob's shadow for as long as anyone can remember. Always second best, always an afterthought."

I considered this new piece of the puzzle as we walked away from the photos. Jonas—overshadowed and resentful—Clara—obsessive and envious—and Jacob, the linchpin to their frustrations, now conspicuously absent.

"I can't help but feel like we're standing on the edge of something more sinister than just a no-show," I said quietly to Thorn.

I turned my attention to Roger, who had sidled up next to us, a grimace on his face that seemed out of place amidst the festivities. "Don't be fooled," he said, his voice tinged with bitterness. "Jacob is ruthless. He'll do anything to win."

I raised an eyebrow, skepticism painting my features. Jacob was competitive, sure, but ruthless? That didn't fit with the man whose work spoke of passion and precision. "That doesn't sound like Jacob Appleton," I replied.

Roger's eyes darkened, and he held up his hand, the scars faint but visible in the low light. "He crushed my hand with a pumpkin two years ago on a TV show. Right before the final carve." His voice was tight, the memory obviously still raw. "I had to have surgery to fix the damage."

Thorn stepped closer, surprising me with his interjection. "I saw that episode," he said, and I could tell he was weighing his words carefully. "It looked like an accident."

Roger's expression shifted, frustration and something akin to resignation battling across his features. He looked between Thorn and me as if deciding how much to push his point.

Thorn maintained eye contact with Roger, unflinching and steady. It was clear he wasn't just speaking as my husband or as the sheriff, he was speaking as someone who had seen the incident in question and had formed his own opinion.

As for me, I couldn't shake off a twinge of unease at Roger's accusation juxtaposed with Thorn's certainty. Accidents happened, especially in high-stress environments like competitions. But what if there was more to it? What if Roger's claim held a kernel of truth?

Roger finally broke the silence that had fallen between us. "Maybe it did look like an accident," he conceded with a heavy sigh. "But when you know Jacob like I do..." His voice trailed off, leaving an implication hanging in the air that refused to be ignored.

I exchanged a glance with Thorn; both of us understood that things were rarely black and white—especially when it came to human emotions and rivalries as deep as these seemed to be.

I listened to Roger's grumble, his voice low and thick with insinuation. "Jacob wanted everyone to believe it was an accident," he muttered, his gaze drifting over the heads of the festivalgoers as if he could spot Jacob among them, hiding in plain sight.

His eyes met mine again, a storm brewing in their depths. "It's not just me Jacob screwed over," he continued, a bitter edge to his words. "Essie... she's got her own beef with him." He paused, his lips pressing into a thin line.

I leaned in, curiosity piqued. "What happened between them?" I prodded gently, hoping he might divulge more.

Roger shook his head, his eyes narrowing. "Let's just say Jacob's good at taking what isn't his." The accusation hung between us, heavy and charged with meaning.

I considered this new information carefully. Essie's recent smile flashed through my mind—too sharp, too satisfied for someone merely enjoying the festival atmosphere. And now Roger was alluding to some dispute she had with Jacob, one that clearly still rankled.

Roger looked away from us then, a clear sign he wasn't going to share anything further. His reluctance to explain left a trail of unanswered questions in its wake. What had happened between Essie and Jacob? What had Jacob allegedly taken from her?

The night air seemed to grow colder as I wrapped my arms around myself. Thorn put an arm around my shoulders.

It was becoming increasingly clear that the competition was more than just about who could carve the best pumpkin—it was about grievances and grudges that ran deep, the kind that could lead to sabotage... or worse.

Jacob's absence gnawed at me even more now. Was it simply a case of cold feet or something more deliberate? With each revelation, the festive lights seemed dimmer and the shadows around us longer.

"We should keep our ears open," I murmured to Thorn. He nodded solemnly, his gaze sweeping across the festival grounds like a lighthouse beam cutting through fog.

"Yes," he agreed quietly. "There's more to this story—more than just an accident or a no-show."

We moved away from Roger then, but the weight of suspicion and half-spoken truths followed us like a second shadow under the harvest moon.

I drifted away from Thorn, drawn to a voice tinged with worry. Martha Thompson's silhouette stood out against the flickering backdrop of jack-o'-lanterns, her hand wringing the hem of her cardigan. "It's turning cutthroat, all this competition," she murmured to a small cluster of listeners who nodded in solemn agreement.

I edged closer, curiosity piqued. "Martha?" I called softly, not wanting to startle her.

She turned, her face creased with lines of concern. "Oh, Kinsley," she greeted me, managing a weary smile. "Just airing some of my worries."

I tilted my head sympathetically. "I overheard you," I confessed. "Do you really think the festival's changed that much?"

Martha sighed, a long exhale that seemed to carry the weight of untold stories. "It used to be about community, you know? Now it's all about winning and getting ahead."

I nodded, understanding the sentiment. The spirit of competition had a way of transforming even the most innocent events into arenas of rivalry.

"Jacob and Jonas have always been at odds," Martha continued, smoothing her cardigan as if to smooth over the tension in her words. "Ever since they were boys." She looked away for a moment before meeting my gaze again. "I always wished they'd get along better—being neighbors and all—but it's just never happened."

The thought of Jacob and Jonas as lifelong rivals painted a vivid picture in my mind—one of two paths diverging from a single point, yet bound by an invisible thread of contention.

"It's gone back that far?" I prodded gently.

Martha nodded. "Oh, yes," she confirmed with a hint of sadness. "It started with small things—races, games... but as they grew older, it became about everything: sports, grades, girls." She paused, her eyes clouding over with memories.

"And now pumpkins," I finished for her.

"Yes." Martha's agreement was faint but firm. "And now pumpkins."

There was something poignant in her acceptance—a resignation to a feud that had outlasted childhood squabbles and matured into something far more complex.

"Is that why you're worried about tonight?" I asked softly.

Martha looked around at the festive decorations that now seemed almost mocking in their cheerfulness. "I just don't want anyone getting hurt—physically or otherwise." Her voice held a tremor that betrayed deeper fears than she was letting on.

"I understand," I said, placing a comforting hand on her shoulder. "We're all hoping for a safe and enjoyable festival."

She managed another weak smile and patted my hand gratefully before excusing herself to mingle with other guests.

As I watched her retreat into the crowd, I couldn't shake the feeling that there were undercurrents here I hadn't even begun to fathom—ripples on the surface that hinted at turbulent depths below. Jacob's absence felt like more than just an empty space; it was a silent alarm bell ringing through the night air. And somewhere between rivalry and resentment lay answers waiting to be unearthed.

I found Thorn again among the throngs of festivalgoers, his eyes scanning faces and body language like he could read the story written there—a story I was becoming increasingly invested in unraveling myself.

Chapter 3

A piercing scream shattered the festival's jovial atmosphere like a glass pumpkin dropped from a great height. Heads turned, bodies tensed. I locked eyes with Thorn, and without a word, we knew the drill. I spun around to my girls, who were wide-eyed with shock.

"Stay with your grandparents," I said, voice steady as I ushered them toward where I saw my parents standing by the cider stand, their faces creased with concern. "Don't move from here, understand?"

They nodded, their usual protests silenced by the urgency in my tone. My father's hand rested on Laney's shoulder, a silent promise of protection.

Once assured of their safety, I turned and sprinted after Thorn. His long strides had already taken him halfway across the fairground toward the source of the commotion. I dodged between clusters of startled festivalgoers, my heart pounding, not just from the exertion but from a gnawing sense of dread.

"Kinsley, go back!" Thorn called over his shoulder as he approached a workshop tucked away behind the rows of booths.

But his command vanished into the crisp autumn air as if carried away by the rustling leaves. I trailed him at a safe distance, enough to give him room to work but close enough to offer assistance if needed. He drew his weapon cautiously and nudged open the door with his boot.

I waited, muscles coiled like a spring, ready to leap into action or cast a protective spell if necessary. The murmurs of the crowd behind me were distant whispers compared to the thudding of my own pulse in my ears as Thorn disappeared into the shadows of the workshop.

Thorn's voice cut through the tension, "All clear!" I swallowed hard, steadying my breath before I stepped into the workshop. The air was thick with the nostalgic scents of pumpkin innards and sawdust, a contradiction to the violence that greeted my eyes. Jacob Appleton sat slumped over his workbench, his body unnaturally still.

I approached hesitantly, my gaze sweeping over the scene. Around him were his creations, pumpkins mid-transformation into masterpieces, their futures as uncertain as Jacob's had been in his final moments. My stomach churned at the sight of him—this man who had breathed life into lifeless gourds now devoid of it himself. And it looked like someone had tried to carve his head like a pumpkin too…

There was an unsettling artistry to the scene; someone had taken their time with him after death. The thought twisted in my gut like a knife. Thorn's hand found my shoulder, a silent comfort amidst the horror.

Penny arrived soon after, her kit in hand and a solemn expression etched on her freckled face. She moved with practiced grace around Jacob, her green eyes sharp and focused. "Blunt force trauma to the back of the head," she announced after a moment, her voice void of emotion—professional detachment.

Thorn and I exchanged a glance. It was a small mercy that Jacob likely hadn't seen it coming, hadn't felt fear or pain in those final seconds.

"The carvings were done postmortem," Penny continued, confirming what we'd feared. "It's sickening, but he didn't suffer from this part." Her hand hovered above Jacob's head without touching— a witch's intuition at work.

I nodded, absorbing her words while fighting back the nausea that threatened to rise. "Who would do something like this?" My voice sounded hollow in my ears.

Penny shrugged slightly as she began to collect samples with meticulous care. "Someone sending a message—or deranged enough to think this is some form of tribute."

The thought sent shivers down my spine. This wasn't just a murder, it was a statement. Thorn stepped away to talk to his deputies, issuing orders with a newfound urgency in his voice.

I lingered near Penny, watching her work while part of me wished I could turn away. But another part— the witch and once-again leader of Coventry Coven— knew I needed to understand this darkness if I was to protect those I loved from it.

The festival outside continued, oblivious to the tragedy that had unfolded within these walls—a reminder that evil often lurked beneath the surface of even the most idyllic scenes.

The workshop was a frozen scene of horror, and I felt like an intruder in a sacred space of grief. My heart clenched at the sight of Jacob, once vibrant and brimming with talent, now reduced to a morbid display. Thorn's silhouette moved like a specter among the shadows, his voice a distant rumble coordinating the aftermath.

Suddenly, Meri darted into the barn, his gold eyes wide with urgency. His sleek black fur stood on end as he weaved through the chaos, his nose twitching as he sniffed around the pumpkins scattered on the floor. His arrival was so sudden, so unexpected that for a moment, I forgot the gruesome scene before me.

"Kinsley," he hissed in that snarky tone that belied his concern. "Here, now."

I knelt beside him, my gaze following his pointed stare to one of the larger pumpkins. Beneath it lay something small and out of place—a charm obscured by shadows and pumpkin debris.

"It's wrong," Meri growled softly. "Feels like a void where there should be light."

His words chilled me. The charm had an unfamiliar symbol etched into its surface—a symbol that seemed to twist and writhe in the dim light of the barn. A knot formed in my stomach; this charm exuded an aura so dark it seemed to swallow the warmth from the air.

"Don't touch it," Meri warned, and I didn't need to be told twice.

I glanced around for something to use, spotting an array of carving tools scattered across a workbench. With care not to disturb any evidence Thorn might need, I selected a pair of tongs and gently slid them under the charm. It seemed to pulse with malevolence as I lifted it from its hiding place.

My hands were steady as I found an empty cardboard box among Jacob's supplies—likely intended for pumpkin scraps or ribbons for winners. Now it would hold something far more sinister. I maneuvered the charm into the box with the tongs, ensuring no part of me made contact with it.

Meri watched intently as I sealed the box, his ears twitching with every rustle of cardboard. "What do you think it means?" I murmured more to myself than to him.

Meri's tail flicked in agitation. "Trouble," he replied succinctly.

The word echoed in my mind as I set the box aside, away from prying eyes but easily accessible for Penny or Thorn to examine later. Trouble had come to Coventry, wrapped in darkness and tucked beneath innocence.

Thorn's steps echoed back to me, his frame emerging from the dance of shadows and light that played across the workshop. "I'm going to talk to some folks who had beef with Jacob," he said, the furrow of his brow deepening with every word. "Want to come along?"

I nodded, gripping the box that now contained the malevolent charm. "Of course." My voice was firmer than I felt. The thought of interviewing suspects, of being a part of the process, it grounded me—gave me a sense of control in a situation that was anything but.

I held up the box slightly, distancing it from my body as if it were radioactive. "I need to put this in the car first," I said, and Thorn's eyes narrowed on the cardboard container.

"What is it?" His question was direct, the sharp edge of concern unmistakable.

"A charm. Found it under one of the pumpkins." I kept my explanation brief, not wanting to delve into the feelings that swirled within me—the sense of dread that had settled in my bones at its discovery. "It's got a bad vibe. Really bad."

Thorn's lips pressed into a thin line as he considered my words. He didn't need to understand magic to recognize when something was off—his instincts as a sheriff had honed his ability to detect when things didn't add up.

"Okay," he said after a pause that seemed to stretch between us like taffy. "Let's secure it."

We moved through the crowd, our path determined and swift. I clutched the box like a dark secret as we navigated between clusters of festivalgoers still unaware of the tragedy that had unfolded mere yards away. The lights from the booths cast colorful shadows on their faces, painting them in shades of ignorance and bliss.

Reaching our car, I placed the box gently in the trunk, as if fearing it might detonate upon impact. The trunk closed with a thud that felt final—a temporary tomb for an object that reeked of malice.

"I don't want to touch it or carry it any longer than necessary," I admitted to Thorn, wiping my hands on my jeans as though I could scrub away the chill that handling the box had left behind.

Thorn's hand found mine, warm and reassuring. "You won't have to," he promised, and for a moment, his touch anchored me in a sea of uncertainty.

With one last glance at the trunk—the barrier between us and whatever darkness resided within—I followed Thorn back into the festival.

Chapter 4

Thorn's hand rested on the small of my back, guiding me through the sea of murmurs and confusion as the festival came to an abrupt halt. Jeremy stood at the exit, a human barrier, his gaze sweeping over the crowd like a lighthouse beam, ensuring no one slipped away unnoticed.

We reached Roger's travel trailer, an island of seclusion amidst the chaos. Thorn knocked with authority—three sharp raps that echoed off the aluminum siding.

"Roger Harris," he called out. "We need a word."

A shuffle inside preceded the door swinging open. Roger appeared in the doorway, his eyes flickering with apprehension. His gaze landed on me and then darted back to Thorn.

"Something happen?" His voice had an edge to it, like a blade too often sharpened.

Thorn tilted his head in a silent invitation to step outside. Roger complied, his frame nearly filling the doorway as he emerged into the dimming light.

"We found Jacob," Thorn said, his voice even but carrying weight. "He's dead."

The news struck Roger like a physical blow. He staggered back a step, hand bracing against the trailer's frame.

"Dead?" He shook his head, disbelief etched into every line of his face. "But how? I mean... who would..."

"Murdered," I added quietly. My eyes searched his face for any flicker of recognition or guilt. Instead, I found shock—raw and unfiltered.

Roger's protective instincts surfaced as he glanced around before asking, "Is Essie okay?"

"She's fine," Thorn assured him. "Right now, we're trying to piece together what happened."

Roger raked a hand through his hair, his thoughts visibly churning. "I was here all day," he offered. "Essie can vouch for me."

"We'll need to speak with her too," Thorn continued methodically. "But tell us about your history with Jacob."

Roger sighed and leaned against the trailer wall, arms crossed over his chest as if shielding himself from more than just the evening chill.

"We had our differences," he admitted. "That TV show... it got heated. But that was two years ago." His eyes met mine, earnest and pleading for understanding. "I'm not a violent man."

Roger's gaze flickered between Thorn and me, a storm of emotions playing across his face as he braced himself against the side of his trailer. Thorn folded his arms, the very picture of patience, but there was a steel edge to his voice that demanded truth.

"Roger, we need to understand the depth of your rivalry with Jacob. The incident on the show—can you walk us through what happened?"

Roger exhaled sharply, his breath visible in the cool air. "It was the night before the finals," he began, his voice tinged with a bitterness that had clearly lingered. "We were all working late, getting our pieces ready. I was moving a heavy pumpkin when it slipped because he ran right into me. It crushed my hand against the table."

"And you believe Jacob did that intentionally?" Thorn pressed, watching Roger's reactions closely.

Roger's hands clenched and unclenched as if reliving the pain. "I saw him nearby, right before it happened. He was smirking, dang it. The way he looked at me... I knew."

Thorn nodded, absorbing every word while I observed Roger's body language—the tension in his shoulders, the tightness around his eyes. It was clear this memory still haunted him.

"But there was no concrete evidence," Thorn pointed out.

"No," Roger admitted, frustration lacing his tone. "It was my word against his. And he played the concerned competitor so well afterward."

Thorn took a step closer, narrowing the distance between them as if trying to bridge into Roger's psyche. "What about after the show? Any confrontations or threats?"

Roger shook his head, but it wasn't in denial—it was in disdain for the thought itself. "I wanted to beat him fair and square, on talent alone. Not by stooping to his level."

I stepped forward then, feeling a pull to contribute to this unraveling narrative. "Did you ever discuss what happened with Jacob after that night?"

His eyes met mine again, and there was a flash of something—a mixture of pain and pride—before he looked away.

"Once," he muttered. "He denied everything. Said it was an accident and that I should let it go." He scoffed lightly, but there was no humor in it. "Let it go—that's rich coming from him."

Thorn gave him a firm nod of acknowledgment before wrapping up. "We'll need to verify your alibi for tonight," he said in a softer tone than before.

"I understand," Roger replied, though he stood taller now as if relieved by having shared his story.

I believed him—there was sincerity in his tone that seemed out of reach for someone capable of such brutality.

Thorn's gaze remained steady, the quintessential lawman dissecting every nuance. "Roger, I hear you that you were with Essie all day. But I need to know where you were at the time of the murder. Where were you before you went onstage?"

Roger shifted, his large hands opening and closing as if he were sculpting the air. "I was here, in my trailer," he said, motioning to the cramped space behind him. "Working on the final touches for tomorrow's competition."

Thorn's brow arched slightly. "And Essie was with you the entire time?"

"Yes," Roger replied, a hint of defensiveness creeping into his voice. "She's been helping me out, learning a lot too. She can vouch for me."

I watched as Thorn considered this information, his mind undoubtedly turning over every possibility. "But you don't have anyone else who can confirm your whereabouts? No one saw you here?"

Roger exhaled, a gust of frustration that seemed to fog up the air between us. "No, I guess not," he admitted, running a hand down his face. "It's just been me and Essie, and she stepped out once or twice to grab some things we needed from town."

The silence hung for a moment as Thorn absorbed Roger's words. I could almost see the wheels turning in his head, questioning the credibility of an alibi so dependent on one person—especially when that person had their own complicated history with Jacob.

Thorn jotted down Roger's words in his notebook, his expression unreadable. He gave a final, assessing look before slipping the pen back into his shirt pocket. "We'll be talking to Essie about tonight," he said with a calm that belied the gravity of the situation. "Just to verify your alibi."

Roger nodded, his posture stiff but cooperative. "Of course. I've got nothing to hide."

"Good to hear," Thorn replied. "And, Roger, stay in town. We might have more questions later."

I watched as Roger's jaw tightened ever so slightly, the muscles working beneath the stubble that shadowed his chin. "I wasn't planning on going anywhere," he assured us.

Thorn's hand found its way back to my back, a silent signal that it was time to move on. As we walked away from Roger's trailer, I felt the tension in the air, thick and sticky like molasses slowing our steps. Thorn's thoughts were elsewhere, likely piecing together the riddle of Jacob's last moments.

We'd find Essie soon enough and see if her story matched Roger's. But for now, there was nothing more to do here.

Chapter 5

The brisk autumn air brushed against my skin as Thorn and I made our way to Essie's trailer. Out of the corner of my eye, I spotted a flash of blonde—a shade too similar to Lisa's hair. My stomach tightened. I turned my head subtly to catch a better glimpse, but the figure melded into the crowd.

Meri, nestled inside my bag, his gold eyes peeking out, whispered, "We've got company."

"I know," I murmured back. "Just caught a glimpse."

Thorn glanced at me, his brow furrowing slightly. He must've sensed my sudden alertness.

"Something wrong?"

"Just thought I saw Lisa," I whispered back, not wanting to alarm him more than necessary. "Meri feels we're being followed."

He scanned the area with his practiced gaze but nodded for us to keep moving. We had a job to do.

We couldn't afford to spook Essie by dealing with Lisa now. A confrontation would alert everyone within earshot, and that included Essie. We needed her unguarded and unsuspecting for this conversation.

"We'll deal with it after," I said, reaching back to squeeze Thorn's hand. His grip was reassuring.

As we approached Essie's trailer, the noises from the festival receded like the tide pulling back from shore. Thorn knocked firmly on the door of the trailer, and we waited in the quiet that followed.

I leaned close to him. "Remember, we're just here for her side of the story."

He nodded once as footsteps sounded from inside. The door swung open and Essie stood before us, her eyes wary but her posture strong.

"Essie Elrod?" Thorn's voice was steady.

"That's me." She tucked a stray strand of hair behind her ear. "What can I do for you, Sheriff?"

"We need to speak to you," Thorn said plainly.

Essie let out a sharp huff of breath. "Come in, I guess."

The interior of Essie's trailer felt cramped, every surface cluttered with sketches of pumpkins and carving tools. She stepped aside, allowing us entry with a stiff nod. Her eyes held a flinty edge, her welcome as chilly as the air outside.

Before Thorn could ease into his questions, Essie's voice cut through the tension. "Jacob was a thief," she declared, arms crossed defiantly over her chest. "But I didn't kill him."

Thorn and I exchanged a quick glance. We settled into the space, careful not to disturb her organized chaos. "We're just trying to understand what happened, Essie," Thorn said, his tone gentle but authoritative.

She scoffed, the sound sharp and bitter. "Understand? He took everything from me—my work, my pride. My hybrid strain was going to change everything for me. Then suddenly his pumpkins started swelling up larger than any mine ever did." She shook her head, a strand of hair falling into her face again.

I stepped closer, trying to soften my presence in the confined trailer. "You think he stole your idea?" My question hung between us like a spider's thread.

"Think? I know he did!" Her voice climbed with each word. "I confronted him about it—demanded compensation and credit. I wanted to file a patent." She laughed without humor, the sound echoing off the metal walls. "But he denied it had anything to do with my pumpkins."

I watched her closely, searching for any flicker of deceit or anger that might betray more than frustration. But all I saw was the raw hurt of betrayal etched into her features—a wound far deeper than mere professional rivalry.

"And you think that's why someone might have wanted to hurt him?" Thorn asked.

Essie's eyes darkened, and she shifted uncomfortably. "People don't kill over pumpkins," she muttered, though it sounded like she was trying to convince herself more than us.

"We've seen stranger motives," Thorn replied calmly.

She met his gaze then and nodded slowly as if conceding his point. "But it wasn't me," she insisted again, her voice steady but tinged with desperation. "I hated what he did, but I didn't kill Jacob."

Thorn nodded, jotting down notes in his small leather-bound book. We needed more than just her word if we were going to clear her name or implicate her in Jacob's death.

I shifted slightly, the space in Essie's trailer confining not just in size but in the tension that filled it. Thorn's presence, usually a comfort, felt almost too large for the room as he leaned in with a question that hung heavy between us.

"Essie, we need to know where you were before we found Jacob's body. Before the introductions onstage," he said, his voice measured and calm.

Essie's eyes darted to mine for a split second before she answered. "I was with Roger, in his trailer. We were prepping for the competition—final touches and all."

Her alibi synced with Roger's earlier claim. But the way she said it, almost too rehearsed, caused a flicker of doubt to snake through my thoughts. I glanced at Thorn to see if he caught it too.

"And you both stayed there until the introductions?" Thorn pressed on.

"Yes," she confirmed with a sharp nod. "We were together the whole time."

Thorn scribbled something in his notebook. I noticed the way Essie held herself—a mix of defensiveness and something else I couldn't quite place.

"The one Jacob didn't show up for," I pointed out, trying to gauge her reaction.

Her lips twisted into a snarky smile. "Yeah, well, he was probably already dead by then."

Thorn's expression hardened just slightly—a subtle shift most wouldn't notice, but I did. "That's likely," he said evenly.

Essie blinked, her bravado slipping for a moment before she shrugged with feigned indifference. "Too bad," she said, her voice cold. "Maybe he got what he deserved for stealing my hard work."

Her words echoed off the walls of the trailer like an accusation left hanging in the air—too pointed, too bitter. It was an unsettling thing to say about someone who'd just been murdered.

Thorn met my eyes, and without speaking a word, we shared the same thought: Essie had motive and resentment in spades. But was it enough to drive her to murder? Or was this just another layer of hurt from a woman who felt wronged?

We needed more than just her words and bitterness; we needed proof and facts. Thorn closed his notebook with a soft snap that seemed to pull Essie back from wherever her thoughts had taken her.

Thorn's notebook closed with a soft finality that seemed to echo in the cramped space of Essie's trailer. Her gaze flitted between us, landing on Thorn with a question unspoken.

"We'll be in touch, Essie," Thorn said, his voice calm but authoritative. "In the meantime, it's important you stay in town."

Her eyes narrowed, the earlier flash of vulnerability gone as quickly as it appeared. "You think I'm a suspect?" The words came out sharp, edged with the same bitterness that had been woven through our entire conversation.

Thorn's posture remained relaxed, but his eyes held firm. "Everyone who had contact with Jacob before his death needs to be available for questioning. It's standard procedure."

I watched her closely, trying to read the tension that seemed to ripple off her like heat from pavement. Was she scared? Angry? It was hard to tell.

"You've got nothing on me," she said defiantly, but there was a tremor in her voice that betrayed her tough exterior.

"We're just following leads, Essie," I chimed in, trying to soften the blow. "We have to consider all possibilities."

She scoffed, crossing her arms tightly across her chest. "Fine. I'm not going anywhere. But you're wasting your time looking at me."

Thorn nodded once and moved toward the door of the trailer. I followed him, sensing his desire to wrap this up cleanly for now.

"Thank you for your cooperation," he said as he stepped out into the fading light of the day.

Essie didn't reply, just watched us with a guarded look as we made our way down the metal steps and onto the grass.

As we walked away from Essie's trailer, I couldn't shake off a feeling of unease. There was something about her certainty, her insistence that she wasn't involved—it felt like there was more beneath the surface than just resentment over stolen pumpkins.

I glanced at Thorn as we put distance between us and the trailers. His jaw was set in that way it always did when he was deep in thought, piecing together a puzzle with missing pieces.

"Think she's telling the truth?" I asked quietly.

He let out a long breath, considering my question. "She believes she is," he finally said. "But belief and truth aren't always one and the same."

The words hung between us as we walked back through the now-silent festival grounds. It was clear we were far from untangling this web; every thread pulled seemed only to tighten the knot further.

For now, all we could do was wait and watch—hope that someone's alibi slipped or another clue surfaced. Until then, everyone remained in limbo, each person a potential piece in this grim mystery.

We'd find out who killed Jacob Appleton—I knew that much for sure. Thorn wouldn't rest until we did. And neither would I.

Chapter 6

A shiver crept along the skin at the base of my skull, the delicate hairs standing on end in the crisp night air as we navigated our path toward the vehicle. Thorn's demeanor was one of strict professionalism, his forehead furrowed with worry, reflecting the somber turn our evening had taken.

"Kinsley," said Meri, his voice a deep, resonant whisper as he materialized from the darkness, "Lisa hasn't left."

My eyes darted across the landscape, taking in the incongruous blend of the carnival's festive illumination and the elongated shadows that the fairground stands threw across the pavement. Then, amidst the chaotic backdrop, my gaze settled on a solitary figure nestled in the branches of a towering oak at the park's edge. It was Lisa, perched precariously on a limb, akin to a raptor under the cover of night, her stare intense and unblinking as it met mine. I couldn't lie, it was creepy.

Noticing the change in my attention, Thorn turned to look and his body tensed. Under his breath, he cursed softly.

Lisa's face drained of color, her ghostly pallor a stark contrast in the dim light as she realized her cover had been blown. In a frantic scramble, she tried to make her way down, her actions marred by haste and fear.

As if betraying her, the branch groaned a foreboding protest before it splintered, unable to support her weight.

With a series of heavy thuds and sharp intakes of breath, she plummeted through the foliage, each collision with the stout branches a harbinger of the fall's end. She finally met the earth with a muffled impact. I tensed, bracing myself to witness the aftermath of a calamitous fall, yet there she was, sprawled amid the scatter of autumnal leaves, her body seemingly unscathed by the ordeal, her expression one of utter disbelief and humiliation.

I caught Thorn's arm, his muscular forearm taut under my grip, as he made to move toward Lisa. She was sprawled awkwardly in the crimson and amber leaves, her fair hair in disarray.

"Wait," I implored, my voice tight with urgency. "I need to talk to her alone."

Thorn's pale eyes, the color of thunderclouds, met mine, a storm brewing within their depths. "Kinsley, she's dangerous," he insisted through gritted teeth. "I can't let you do that. As an officer of the law, I need to arrest her."

Frustration knotted my chest as we stood at an impasse. "Thorn, please, she won't say anything with you there intimidating her. I might be able to coax some information out of her." I kept my tone gentle but firm.

His jaw set stubbornly. "Not a chance," he retorted, his hand resting on his hip. "I'm not letting you put yourself in harm's way with that...that crazy woman." He nearly spat the words.

While we locked horns under the eaves of the forest, neither willing to yield, Lisa had regained her composure. With the cunning and wariness of a cornered animal sensing an opportunity, she seized the moment. She was on her feet in an instant, leaves clinging to her sweater and jeans, and darted into the shadows before either of us could react.

"Dammit!" Thorn cursed vehemently, immediately sprinting after her fleeing silhouette.

I followed suit but it was futile; Lisa vanished swiftly between the trees like smoke caught on an autumn wind. We were no match for her knowledge of the terrain.

Panting, we stumbled to a halt in a small, moonlit clearing, Thorn kicking violently at the dirt in frustration. "We should have worked together to apprehend her," he growled.

I threw my hands up in exasperation, my ponytail coming loose. "That's what I was trying to do!" I cried. "If you had just listened..."

Our eyes locked as we stood under the starry sky—a silent acknowledgment passing between us that we both wanted the same outcome.

Thorn ran a hand through his wind-mussed, unruly hair and sighed. "This is getting us nowhere tonight," he admitted wearily. "She's gone, and we don't know where. I could try her parents' house… or we could knock on her old friends' doors, but… And then I still need to talk to the other witnesses. I don't think I have time for both."

I gazed back in the direction of the harvest festival grounds, now a chaotic crime scene swarmed by the local deputies. The weight of this long and difficult day pressed down heavily on my shoulders. "You're right," I agreed softly. "The other witnesses can wait until tomorrow. It's getting late now anyway. And there's no point in going on a wild goose chase for Lisa either. I'm sure she'll show herself again. No need to chase her."

I gently touched his arm in a consoling gesture. Wordlessly, he placed his large hand over mine, gratefully accepting the unspoken comfort.

Thorn cast one last conflicted glance over his shoulder towards the festival grounds, his handsome face a mask of dogged concern and duty. But then he looked down at me again and something softened in his stormy eyes. "Yeah," he conceded with a small, tired smile, "let's head home."

***

I leaned my head against the cool glass of the passenger side window, watching the nighttime scenery pass by in a blur as Thorn drove us home. Despite the lateness of the hour, I couldn't relax - my mind churned endlessly with the disturbing events of the evening. First the gruesome murder of poor Jacob, his body torn apart in a way that turned my stomach. And then there was the unnerving encounter with Lisa lurking in the shadows, her intent clearly malicious.

A heavy gloom seemed to settle over me, weighing down my limbs and even my thoughts. It was an effort just to keep my eyes open. From my lap, Meri let out a miserable mewl, the usually snarky cat uncharacteristically despondent. "I don't feel so good either," Meri groused, his ears flattened against his head.

"You okay, Kins?" Thorn asked, glancing over at me with concern etched across his handsome features, his stormy eyes clouded with worry.

"I don't know..." I murmured. "I just feel...sad all of a sudden. And so tired. I was just wondering if anything even means anything anymore..." My voice trailed off as I stared sightlessly out the window, a profound sense of hopelessness threatening to swallow me whole.

Meri meowed again, the sound weak and pathetic, so unlike his normal sarcastic self. "It seems so hopeless all of a sudden. I have no idea why."

"I think it's that charm from the crime scene," I realized aloud, my sluggish mind struggling to make sense of things. "It must be cursed or something. Can you drive faster?"

Thorn pressed down on the gas pedal, the engine revving in response. "Hang in there. We're almost home." His tone was gentle but urgent.

I nodded slightly, too depleted to even respond. The further we drove with the cursed box in the trunk, the darker my thoughts became. By the time we pulled into the driveway, well, I would never admit out loud the truly bleak things that had run through my mind on that short car ride.

Meri hopped out of the car the moment I opened the door, shaking himself as if to dispel the last remnants of the charm's malevolent energy. "That thing is bad news," he declared with a shudder, his fur standing on end. "It feels like death."

The cool night air felt refreshing against my skin as I stepped out of the car, a welcome reprieve from the oppressive aura of the cursed object. The dark cloud that had settled over my mind already began to dissipate, though a lingering unease remained coiled in my core.

Thorn retrieved the cardboard box from the trunk, handling it with care despite its innocuous appearance. Still, as he drew nearer, an insidious chill crept over me once more. This thing was dangerous; we had to destroy it.

"Let's get this over with," I said grimly, steeling myself as we approached the ancient hangman's tree looming in the front yard. Its gnarled branches seemed to reach for the box greedily.

Thorn set the box down and withdrew his phone, snapping a few photos from various angles. He also took a brief video, documenting the strange symbol etched into the charm's surface - our only clue as to its origins. I shifted my weight from foot to foot impatiently. The longer I stood near it, the more its dark energy crept into my mind like poisonous tendrils.

Finally finished, Thorn stepped back. "Do what you have to do," he told me with a nod, his expression somber. He knew the danger magical objects could pose.

Meri sat back on his haunches, his eyes glowing in the moonlight. "On three?" he asked. I nodded, rolling up my sleeves and concentrating on summoning my power. Meri did the same, his fur standing on end as energy crackled around us.

"One…" I began, the wind picking up as if responding to our mounting power.

"Two…" Meri growled, baring his teeth at the insidious thing.

"Three!" I cried, unleashing a torrent of light magic just as Meri let loose a blast of fire. Our combined powers slammed into the box with a resounding crack, obliterating it in a blinding flash. The tainted charm dissolved into ash, its dark energy dispelled by our light.

Panting, I brushed my windswept hair from my face. An immense relief flooded through me as the last remnants of the cursed object's influence evaporated. Nearby, Meri sat back on his haunches looking immensely pleased with himself.

"Well, that's done," he purred smugly.

I let out a shaky laugh. "Yes, thank goodness." I turned to Thorn, who was regarding the scorched earth with a look of satisfaction. "I don't know who created that foul thing, but I have a bad feeling they're involved with the murder."

Thorn's expression turned grim, the lines on his face deepening. "I agree."

***

I let out a long sigh as I sank into the plush couch cushions, the tension in my shoulders slowly unwinding. Thorn joined me a moment later, wrapping a strong arm around my shoulders and drawing me close. I nestled against his side, breathing in his familiar woodsy scent and already feeling the lingering unease from the cursed charm beginning to fade.

"I'm sorry about earlier," I murmured, glancing up at him. "I should have listened to you with Lisa. We're partners, we need to work together."

Thorn's expression softened, his stormy eyes gentle. "It's all right, love. We were both on edge after everything that happened tonight." He pressed a kiss to my temple. "I know you just wanted to protect everyone. That's one of the things I admire most about you."

I gave him a small smile, comforted by his words. He always knew how to make me feel better.

We sat in easy silence for a few minutes, simply taking comfort in each other's presence. The only sounds were the old house gently creaking and Meri's rumbling purrs from his spot at our feet.

Eventually, I broke the quiet. "Do you think we'll be able to figure out who killed Jacob?" I asked. "I know you said the investigation will take time, but I have a bad feeling the murderer could strike again."

Thorn considered for a moment before responding. "I honestly don't know yet if it was a crime of passion or premeditated. But now that we have some leads, I'm hopeful we can get to the bottom of this soon."

He absently ran his fingers through my hair. "Try not to worry too much tonight. You've been through enough stress already today. I know it's hard when someone is threatening our town, but we'll find them."

I nodded, knowing he was right. I just hated feeling powerless, but obsessing over the case wouldn't do any good right now.

"You're right," I conceded. "I'll try to let it go for now." I paused, then added teasingly, "Distract me?"

A roguish grin spread across Thorn's face. "I think I can manage that."

Chapter 7

Rising with the sun, I was filled with a sense of purpose, driven to delve into the mysteries of the enigmatic charm that lay among the evidence of the crime scene. Its aura of dark magic was a silent alarm, prompting an urgent need to unravel its origins and intentions. Yet, in the stark light of day, I was struck by the realization of my inadequate resources. The devastating fire that consumed my shop had also devoured most of my treasured occult tomes. The daunting task of sifting through the charred remains of my once vibrant establishment remained untouched; the emotional toll of the catastrophe made it unbearable to confront the shattered remnants of my life's work. The promise of an insurance payout lingered in administrative limbo, and the thought of reconstructing what was lost seemed like an insurmountable feat. The wounds were too fresh, the heartache too acute. Moreover, my magical reserves were severely depleted – the aftermath of the harrowing "Meri incident" had left me with little strength to rebuild through supernatural means.

As the morning light cast a warm glow across the room, I found myself nursing a cup of coffee, gazing pensively through the window. There must exist some avenue, some untapped source of knowledge, that could cast light on the mystery of the charm. The destruction of my shop would not derail the quest for truth. Jacob's memory demanded it.

With renewed determination, I resolved to explore the dusty shelves of my attic library following breakfast. I had previously transferred what I assumed were the most crucial volumes to my shop, yet it was possible that some overlooked gem remained hidden within my home. The charm was an important lead, a whispering echo of the perpetrator, and it was imperative that it not become yet another dead end. Should the attic yield no answers, then the town library would be my next stop. Though its magical collection paled compared to the breadth and depth of my personal archive, there might still be a glimmer of insight nestled among its public stacks.

I smiled at my daughters as they bounded down the stairs, their youthful exuberance momentarily lifting my spirits. "Good morning, girls," I greeted them warmly as I finished preparing their breakfast.

Laney's blonde hair bounced as she slid into her seat. "Mom, who was that man that died yesterday?" she asked curiously. I hesitated, not wanting to expose them to the grim details.

"Don't you worry about that, sweetie," I said gently. "The police are handling it."

Hekate piped up from across the table. "That's what Grandma said too when we asked her last night."

I chuckled knowingly. "Well, your Grandma is very wise, so you should listen to her." It warmed my heart that my mother was there for my girls when I couldn't be.

Laney took a big bite of toast before asking, "Can we stay at Grandma's tonight? Since she dropped us off last night and we didn't get to stay?"

I smiled indulgently. "It's fine by me if Grandma says it's okay." The thought of them safe with my mother gave me comfort.

We finished up breakfast and I walked the girls out to the bus stop, the morning sun casting everything in a cheerful glow. I waved as the bus pulled away, then a rustling sound from the trees across the street caught my attention. I stared hard at the trees surrounding the old cemetery, thinking I saw a figure dart behind one of them just as I looked.

"Did you see that, Meri?" I asked. The big black cat peered intently at the area.

"I don't know," he reported. We crossed the street to investigate, but found no trace of the lurker. Still, the encounter left me unsettled. What were they doing at the cemetery?

"We should go up to the attic and see what we can find about that charm," I told Meri as we went back across the street.

"If we have to," he groused as we walked into the house.

I headed up the creaky attic stairs, Meri padding along behind me. Dust motes danced in the shafts of morning light streaming through the small windows. I paused for a moment to take in the sight of the attic library that I hadn't visited in ages. The old bookshelves lined the walls, packed tightly with leather-bound tomes, ancient scrolls, and curious artifacts. This collection represented generations of magical knowledge, spanning centuries.

"Well, Meri, let's see if we can find anything useful about that wretched charm," I said, stepping further into the room. As I scanned the shelves, pondering where to begin, a book tumbled off the top shelf, landing at my feet with a muffled thump. I bent to pick it up, brushing dust off the cover. "Curses and Charms of the Ancient World," I read. "How fortuitous." I flashed a grin at Meri.

Settling into an old armchair nestled between the shelves, I cracked open the heavy book. Meri hopped up onto my lap, peering curiously at the faded pages as I turned them. "Here it is," I murmured excitedly, my finger landing on an illustration that was a precise match to the etched symbol on the charm. "A Misery Curse, intended to plunge the victim into despair through malicious psychic assault." My brow furrowed as I read the description, a chill running through me at the thought of such dark magic being unleashed on poor Jacob.

I picked up my phone and dialed Thorn's number, eager to share what I had discovered about the sinister charm.

"Hey, honey," he answered, his warm voice instantly making me smile despite the grim context of my call.

"Hi, Thorn, I found something important in the attic this morning," I began. "That charm from the crime scene? It's something called a Misery Curse, meant to inflict psychic despair on the victim."

Thorn let out a low whistle. "Wow, that's dark stuff. Good work tracking that down, and I think that proves the murder was premeditated and not a crime of passion."

"Have there been any other developments?" I asked.

"I've got Jonas Thompson coming in this afternoon to be interviewed. He's the neighbor with the long-standing rivalry with Jacob. Since you're already looped in on this case with the charm, do you want to observe the interview?"

"Absolutely," I replied without hesitation.

"Great, stop by the station around 2:00 p.m. then," Thorn said. "With any luck, Jonas will let something slip that gives us a solid lead."

"I hope so," I sighed. "The sooner we can unravel this mystery, the better. Jacob deserves justice."

"Don't worry, we'll get to the bottom of this," Thorn reassured me, his steadfast determination evident even through the phone.

We exchanged goodbyes and I ended the call, placing my phone down on the side table next to my chair. The old book still lay open to the page detailing the Misery Curse. I shivered, unsettled by the malicious intent behind such magic. What bitter rivalry or festering grudge could drive someone to inflict such torment?

* * *

I sat behind the one-way glass, watching as my husband questioned our prime suspect. Jonas Thompson fidgeted in his seat, glancing around nervously as Thorn laid out the details of Jacob's murder.

"Let's talk about your relationship with the victim," Thorn said, steepling his fingers on the metal table between them. "You were neighbors, competitors...some might even say rivals."

Jonas scoffed. "We were hardly rivals. Jacob always won those pumpkin contests, year after year. Wasn't much of a competition if you ask me."

"Yet you kept entering, kept trying to beat him." Thorn flipped open the case file, scanning a sheet of paper. "Says here you've come in second place to Jacob for the past five years straight."

"So what? It was just a little friendly competition between neighbors." Jonas shrugged, but his jaw clenched. "Doesn't mean I killed the guy."

Thorn regarded him steadily. "No, but it does suggest a motive. After all those years in Jacob's shadow, watching him take home prize after prize, I can imagine you'd be pretty resentful."

Jonas shifted in his seat. "Maybe a little, but nothing worth killing over." His eyes darted around again. "I don't know anything about what happened to him."

"Is that so?" Thorn pulled out a plastic evidence bag and placed it on the table. Inside was an ornate knife with what looked like bloodstains on the blade. "We found this among the pumpkin carving tools in the workshop. The blood matches Jacob's DNA. Is this yours?"

Jonas paled. "I don't know whose knife that is. I swear, I didn't hurt Jacob!" His composure was cracking. "It's certainly not mine!"

Thorn leaned forward intently. "I think you got tired of losing to him. You saw this contest, with the big cash prize, as your chance to finally beat Jacob. But you knew you couldn't do it fair and square, could you?"

"No, I - I would never -" Jonas stammered.

"So you killed him. Got him out of the way so you could take first prize without him around. Then you tried to send a message by carving up his corpse." Thorn's stare was icy. "How am I doing so far?"

Jonas looked trapped, glancing between Thorn and the apparent murder weapon. Finally, his shoulders slumped in defeat. "All right, yes, I was jealous of Jacob," he admitted. "Maybe I wished he would fail, lose just once. But I didn't kill him, I swear it!"

He seemed sincere, but was he telling the truth? I studied his face, searching for any deception. If he was the killer, we needed to get to the bottom of this pumpkin rivalry, and fast.

Jonas fidgeted under Thorn's steady gaze, clearly nervous, but he never cracked. He admitted to feeling resentful over always losing to Jacob but swore up and down he didn't kill the man. Thorn pushed and prodded, even produced the apparent murder weapon found with Jacob's blood on it. But Jonas vehemently denied it was his or that he was involved.

"I wanted to beat him fair and square, not kill him!" Jonas insisted, hands splayed on the table. "You gotta believe me, I had nothing to do with this!"

Watching his face, I didn't see any of the usual tells of deception. He seemed earnest, even rattled. But was he telling the truth?

Finally, Thorn had to let him go, without any solid evidence tying him to the crime scene. As Jonas hurried out, Thorn came to meet me, frustration etched on his handsome face.

"He's our top suspect, but I can't break his story," Thorn admitted. "There's got to be more to this pumpkin rivalry than he's saying. We're missing something here."

I nodded, thoughtful. Jonas hadn't struck me as a killer, but there was definitely bad blood between him and Jacob. We needed to get to the bottom of it, and find out if Jonas's jealousy really did turn deadly. But how? There had to be a lead we were overlooking. Some secret or piece of history between the two men that would reveal if Jonas had a motive to commit murder after all.

Thorn's steps echoed through the sterile hallway, matching the rhythm of my own. He seemed lost in thought, no doubt turning over every word Jonas Thompson had uttered in the interrogation room.

The crease between his brows spoke volumes of his frustration.

"Kinsley, I can't shake the feeling we're dancing around the truth," he muttered as we approached his office. "Jonas is hiding something, but I can't put my finger on it."

I nodded, about to respond, when a commotion at the front desk drew our attention. There stood Clara Greenway, her cheeks flushed with anger and her eyes ablaze. The sight of her stopped me cold.

"Jonas didn't do anything wrong!" Clara's voice sliced through the air like a shard of ice. "You need to leave him alone!"

The deputies at the desk were trying to calm her, but she was having none of it. Her fists were balled at her sides, and she looked ready to take on anyone who got in her way.

Thorn's hand lightly touched my back, nudging me to stay put as he moved toward the ruckus. "Clara," he called out firmly yet calmly, asserting his presence without escalating tensions.

She spun around, hair whipping like a fiery lash. Her eyes locked onto Thorn's with an intensity that made me shiver despite myself.

"If Jonas did anything to Jacob," Clara spat out, "it was for me!"

The statement hung heavy in the air, and every head in the station turned toward us. Thorn didn't hesitate. "Jeremy, hold Jonas," he called out without taking his eyes off Clara. Jonas, who had almost made it out of the building, was stopped in his tracks.

"Clara Greenway," he said in that same level tone that always managed to get people to listen, "you need to come with me."

Without waiting for her response, Thorn guided Clara by the elbow into a smaller interrogation room adjacent to his office. I trailed behind them, my mind racing.

Did Clara just imply she had something to do with Jacob's murder? And if so, how deep did this tangled web of love and jealousy go? I stepped into the observation room just as Thorn closed the door behind himself, sealing himself in with a woman whose next words might just blow this case wide open while I watched.

Chapter 8

I leaned in to peer through the glass of the observation window, I couldn't tear my eyes away from Clara. There she sat, her discomfort obvious as she squirmed in the chair facing Thorn. Her fingers, seemingly of their own accord, twisted and toyed with the fabric of her shirt, while her voice betrayed the occasional quiver—undeniable signs of distress. I had borne witness to countless guilty parties throughout my career; Clara's behavior fit the classic pattern.

Thorn mirrored her forward lean, his demeanor serene, yet his tone carried an unmistakable edge of urgency. "Clara, there was a particular statement you made earlier that piqued my curiosity. You suggested that if Jonas had hurt Jacob, it would be on your behalf. Can you elaborate on that?"

Clara's eyes, wide with a mix of fear and possibly desperation, flicked to Thorn. "I... I didn't mean anything by it," she faltered. "Jonas is... he's inherently kindhearted. He's not the type to hurt anybody."

"But you're suggesting he could be driven to extremes to safeguard someone he cares about?" Thorn continued to probe, his intense gaze locking with hers in a silent challenge.

"Yes, but not— Not in the way you're implying." Clara's voice splintered, a clear sign of her inner turmoil, and she inhaled a shuddering breath, seemingly an attempt to fortify her resolve. "He's not a murderer. His actions are driven by compassion, nothing more."

I found myself angling my head slightly, my eyes narrowing as I dissected her every twitch and gesture. Beneath the veneer of her frantic protests lay a deeper truth she was hesitating to reveal. Thorn's keen perception was attuned to this as well; his talent for deciphering human behavior was almost uncanny.

"Clara," his voice dropped to a whisper, tender and persuasive as if to gently unravel the truth from her lips, "is there a particular concern gnawing at you? Is there a reason you believe Jonas might feel compelled to step in to defend you?"

Her gaze plummeted back to her restless hands, and she appeared on the verge of being crushed by the burden of her own concealed truths. However, she mustered a vehement shake of her head.

"No," her voice was barely audible, a breathy denial. "No, I'm convinced he's not responsible for Jacob's death."

As I watched Clara from behind the one-way mirror, a knot tightened in my stomach. The fluorescent lights overhead cast a harsh glow on her pale face, highlighting the raw emotion etched into her features.

I leaned closer, my breath fogging up a small patch of the glass.

Thorn leaned back in his chair, his gaze never wavering from Clara's face. "Clara, tell me about Jacob's work. How did it influence you?"

Her eyes lit up for a fraction of a second before clouding over with something dark and complex. "Jacob was... is a genius," she started, her voice laced with reluctant admiration. "His work was something I looked up to—no, aspired to surpass."

"And did that drive you? This need to be better than him?" Thorn's question was like a scalpel, precise and probing.

Clara nodded, a rush of color flooding her cheeks. "Yes," she confessed, her voice barely above a whisper. "It consumed me. I spent every waking hour trying to think of ways to carve better, to innovate... to win."

"Did this obsession cause any issues between you and Jonas?" Thorn's question seemed casual, but I could hear the underlying steel.

A frown creased Clara's forehead as she hesitated. Her hands clenched in her lap, betraying her inner conflict. "Jonas... he didn't always understand my passion," she admitted with a tinge of defensiveness creeping into her tone.

I could see the realization dawning in her eyes as she spoke—each word inadvertently painting Jonas in a darker shade. She seemed to shrink back into herself as if wanting to physically retract what she had just revealed.

Abruptly, she clamped her mouth shut, her lips forming a tight line. The room fell silent except for the faint hum of the air conditioning. Clara sat frozen, as if any further words might condemn not just Jonas but herself as well.

I stepped back from the window and took a deep breath, trying to quell the unease bubbling inside me. Clara's last sentence hung heavy in the air—a potent reminder that sometimes obsession could drive people to do the unthinkable.

Thorn told Clara to hold tight for a few minutes, his brow furrowed with frustration. He caught my eye and motioned for me to join him in the hallway. I pushed off the wall, feeling the tension in my shoulders as I made my way to meet him.

"What do you think?" he asked as soon as I was within earshot, his voice low.

I crossed my arms, considering Clara's erratic behavior. "She's hiding something," I murmured. "Her admiration for Jacob's work... it borders on obsession."

He nodded, his expression grave. "And obsession can drive people to extreme measures."

We shared a look. Clara's desire to eclipse Jacob in the carving world could be a potent motive, but conjecture wasn't enough to hold her.

"Still," I continued, "it's not sufficient evidence to detain her or Jonas. Without something concrete tying them to the crime scene or Jacob's death..."

Thorn sighed, running a hand through his hair. "I know. We can't hold them based on speculation."

My mind raced with the possibilities—each more troubling than the last. Clara had revealed just enough to paint herself into a corner but not enough for an arrest.

"We need to keep digging," I said decisively. "Someone out there knows more than they're letting on."

He glanced back at the door to the interrogation room where Clara waited, uncertainty etched into her face even through the window.

"I'll let them go," he said with a hint of reluctance. "But we'll keep a close eye on both of them."

I gave him a nod, trusting his judgment despite the gnawing sense that we were missing a crucial piece of this twisted tapestry.

As Thorn went back into the room to release Clara, and then Jonas, I stood alone in the hallway, my thoughts churning. Whoever was responsible for Jacob's death had left us grasping at shadows.

* * *

The room had a stale air of formality as Ted Mellon settled into the chair across from Thorn. The fluorescent lights hummed above, casting a harsh glow on his Botox-smooth face. He fiddled with his shirt cuffs, betraying a hint of unease beneath his polished exterior.

I leaned back against the wall, arms crossed. Thorn's presence filled the space between us, his posture relaxed but attentive. His notebook lay open on the table, a pen poised in his hand.

"Ted, thanks for coming in," Thorn began, his voice steady and inviting.

"Of course, Sheriff Wilson," Ted replied with a practiced smile. "Happy to help however I can."

Thorn nodded, jotting down a note before looking up again. "We're trying to piece together Jacob's last day. Did you notice anything unusual at the festival?"

Ted shook his head. "It was all pretty standard fare until... well, you know." He gestured vaguely in the air as if to brush away the gravity of Jacob's death.

"And the competitors? Any interactions with Jacob that stood out?" Thorn prodded gently.

Ted paused, tapping his finger on the table. "Actually, yes. I saw Jonas and Jacob having a pretty heated argument by the pumpkin display. Not sure what about, but they were at each other's throats."

Thorn scribbled down another note. "Do you recall when this was?"

"Day before last, mid-afternoon." Ted glanced at me briefly before returning his focus to Thorn.

"Was anyone else present during this altercation?"

Ted furrowed his brow in thought. "An older woman stepped in—broke it up." He looked off into space as if trying to conjure her image from memory.

"Can you describe her?" Thorn asked.

"She had this soft, silvery gray hair that shone almost white when the sun hit it. Fell loosely past her shoulders in waves. Pretty heart-shaped face with these dancing green eyes, cute little nose with some faded freckles, and deep red lips.

"Wore one of those crazy hand-knit orange sweaters with a black cat poking out the front pocket. Had on this flowing purple skirt too, layers of tulle peeking out under it. Rainbow socks visible over some black ankle boots made to look like gnomes or something.

"And get this - she had an apron on with dancing skeletons all over it. Had some smudges on it of either cocoa powder from baking cookies or dirt from gardening. Like she'd just wandered out of her kitchen or greenhouse without thinking to change.

"She had a necklace too of tiny little silver spoons, and these big glasses. I gotta say, she seemed like some kind of quirky fairy godmother who just stepped out of a storybook. One of those creative, magical types you know? Just unexpectedly standing there on the sidewalk in front of me."

Ted chuckled, scratching his head of messy brown hair. "She was something else. It's all still a bit hazy to me, but I definitely won't be forgetting that colorful character anytime soon."

My mind immediately sketched Martha Thompson's figure: always wearing her apron like armor, ready to tend to her son or her pumpkin patch at a moment's notice.

"That sounds like Martha Thompson," I murmured without realizing I'd spoken aloud. "Jonas's mother."

Thorn shot me a quick glance and then turned back to Ted. "Anything else you remember about their fight?"

"Just that it was intense." Ted shrugged helplessly. "I try to stay out of these local squabbles."

Thorn closed his notebook with a soft thud and stood up. "Thank you for your time, Ted."

As Ted left the room, relief seemed to lift him slightly taller than when he'd entered. Thorn turned to me with determination etched in his features.

"We need to talk to Martha next," he said firmly.

I nodded in agreement, feeling the puzzle pieces shift and slide into place as we delved deeper into the heart of Coventry's pumpkin rivalry and its dark harvest of secrets.

Chapter 9

The ride to Jonas's place stretched ahead, the atmosphere a mix of tension and silent contemplation. Thorn gripped the steering wheel, eyes scanning the road, his mind clearly dissecting every piece of information we'd collected so far. I was nestled in the passenger seat, fingers tracing the window's edge, lost in thought about the charm and what other secrets Coventry might be hiding.

A sharp ring cut through the silence as Thorn's phone buzzed with urgency. He glanced at the caller ID and answered. "Sheriff Wilson here."

Dispatch relayed information that made Thorn's brow furrow and his grip on the wheel tighten. "Roger Harris? What—hang on." He threw a quick look my way, his voice full of disbelief and concern. "We're on our way."

"What happened?" I asked, my heart thudding against my ribcage.

"Roger tried to end it," Thorn said grimly. "With a pumpkin vine, of all things."

My breath caught. The image was grotesque, almost poetic in its twisted irony—a carver entangled by the very emblem of his craft.

We rerouted to the fairgrounds, Thorn pushing the speed limit as much as he dared. The setting sun cast an orange glow over everything, giving a picturesque yet eerie backdrop to our urgent drive.

The fairgrounds were quiet when we arrived, save for the fluttering tape marking off areas and the occasional rustle of leaves in the breeze. We parked near the RV park, where portable sheds had been erected as temporary workshops for visiting carvers.

I spotted an ambulance parked haphazardly outside one of these sheds, paramedics bustling around. Roger lay on a stretcher just outside his assigned shed. His face was pale, haunted by whatever demons had driven him to such despair.

Thorn was out of the car before I fully processed what was happening. He moved with a purposeful stride toward Roger and the paramedic team attending him. I followed close behind, feeling a swell of pity for Roger. The competition, his feelings for Essie, Jacob's death—it had all converged into a perfect storm that nearly claimed him.

I caught snippets of conversation as paramedics worked around him.

"Found him just in time," one said.

"Barely breathing when we cut him down," another added.

Thorn stood beside Roger, who looked dazed but alive—thank goodness for small mercies. "Roger," Thorn said gently but firmly. "Can you tell me what happened?"

Roger's eyes fluttered open; they were red-rimmed and vacant. His lips moved but no sound came out at first. When he finally spoke, his voice was hoarse, barely above a whisper.

"I couldn't... I didn't..." His words trailed off into sobs.

Roger, a man whose hands shaped beauty from the mundane, now lay crumpled and hollow-eyed on a stretcher. His neck bore angry red marks, stark against his pale skin. The air buzzed with the electricity of fear and confusion, paramedics moving with practiced urgency.

Thorn's face was etched with concern. "Roger," he repeated, steadying the shaken carver with a firm hand on his shoulder.

Roger's gaze locked onto Thorn's. "The vine... it broke," he said, each word a struggle to push past his lips. "I don't know what happened... what came over me." His eyes wandered as if searching the sky for answers that refused to descend.

"I was just carving," Roger continued, voice quivering like a leaf in the wind. "Practicing for the competition—it's all I wanted to focus on." He paused, swallowing hard as if the words themselves were bitter pills. "Then this dark cloud just... just rolled over me."

My heart raced as I watched him.

"I couldn't see any hope," Roger whispered, his voice trailing into the cool evening air. "It felt like I might as well end it now."

Thorn's hand tightened on Roger's shoulder—a comforting gesture, spurring him to go on.

"When the vine broke," Roger went on, "I snapped out of it enough to stumble outside." A shudder ran through him at the memory. "And then... I felt better. Just like that."

Thorn and I exchanged a glance, and in that brief connection, unspoken understanding passed between us. He must've been piecing together the same thing I was—the charm I obliterated last night, its sinister influence, the way it had wrapped its tendrils around our minds. The timing was too coincidental, Roger's sudden plunge into despair mirroring the effects of that cursed object.

He leaned in close to Roger, his voice a blend of authority and empathy. "You're going to the hospital to get checked out," Thorn instructed firmly. His hand patted Roger's arm in a reassuring manner, grounding him back to the present.

Turning to the EMTs, Thorn's tone dropped to a whisper meant only for their ears. "Keep an eye on him," he advised discreetly. "I don't think he needs a psych hold." His eyes met mine again with a glint of doubt, knowing full well that call wasn't ours to make, but he had to try. Job experience told him that the emergency room staff would listen to the EMTs.

Roger nodded weakly, the fight drained from him like water from a punctured pail. As they loaded him into the ambulance, I watched the paramedics secure him with straps and blankets—for his safety and comfort.

Thorn and I stood side by side as the ambulance doors closed, its siren slicing through the quiet evening as it departed. We remained there for a moment longer than necessary, lost in our thoughts. It was clear now; we were dealing with something that stretched beyond mere human malice. A chill ran down my spine as I considered what other shadows might be lurking unseen, waiting to tighten their grip on unsuspecting souls.

As the ambulance faded into the distance, I inhaled deeply, bracing myself to step into the shed where Roger's despair had reached its peak. The air was thick with the day's waning warmth, carrying the scent of freshly carved pumpkins and hay. Meri stirred in my bag, his weight shifting as if he too sensed the gravity of what we were about to face.

We entered Roger's shed, and immediately, a shiver raced up my spine. The atmosphere was heavy, charged with an invisible weight that pressed down on my chest. Meri's ears flattened against his head, a low growl vibrating from his throat.

"Feel that?" I murmured to him.

"Like walking into a spider's web," he replied with a hiss. His eyes scanned the room, alert and wary.

I moved slowly through the shed, past shelves laden with carving tools and sketches of pumpkin designs that would never see fruition. My gaze swept over the scattered hay around the workbench, and there it was—a shadow amid the ordinary, a blot of darkness that seemed to suck in the light.

"There," I pointed out to Thorn. "Underneath the hay."

Thorn approached cautiously and pushed aside the hay with a gloved hand. The charm revealed itself, a twisted piece of metal inscribed with symbols that seemed to dance and flicker in the fading light.

I held my breath as Thorn picked it up. He examined it closely but showed no sign of distress—no flinch, no grimace. "Looks like another one of those charms," he said calmly.

Meri poked his head out from my bag, eyeing Thorn with suspicion. "Not feeling woozy or contemplating your own demise?"

Thorn shook his head. "Nope. Feels like just a piece of metal to me."

That confirmed it—the charm only targeted those sensitive to magic or who harbored magic within themselves. It made sense now; these charms were like silent predators lying in wait for prey with an inherent connection to magic—prey like Roger and me.

"We can't keep this wretched thing," I said gravely, meeting Thorn's eyes. "It's far too dangerous – this charm feeds voraciously on magic. It will only hurt more innocent people if we don't get rid of it now."

Thorn's dark brows knitted together, reluctance written in the set of his stubbled jaw. As an officer sworn to uphold the law, evidence was evidence to him, even if it was of the supernatural variety. But over the years, he had come to trust my judgment implicitly when it came to matters of magic and the unseen forces at work in our strange little town of Coventry.

With a resigned sigh that lifted his broad shoulders, he pulled out his phone and methodically snapped several photos of the metal charm from different angles. His face was illuminated by the screen's sterile glow in the dim light of the shed. Once satisfied with thoroughly documenting it, he gave me a single grim nod.

"All right, Kinsley. Do what you have to do." His voice was low and taut.

I steeled myself as I leaned down, my hair slipping over my shoulder. Meri hissed softly in warning from next to my feet. The charm exuded an aura that prickled menacingly against my senses - sinister energy, ravenous and parasitic. This close, its pull was almost hypnotic, dredging up my own doubts and fears that I would rather leave buried deep in the recesses of my mind.

Shaking off its cloying effects, I conjured a glowing sphere of cleansing light in my palms, muttering the words of power. The charm seemed to recoil from my magic, oily shadows swirling violently across its engraved surface as it was revealed in its true nature. With an effort that made my palms burn, I unleashed the purifying energy in a targeted blast and fully engulfed the vile object.

An unearthly, unnatural shriek pierced the stuffy air of the shed as the charm disintegrated in a flash of blazing white fire, leaving only traces of blackened ash and echoes of malice. I slumped back against a bale of hay, drained but profoundly relieved to have neutralized another threat oozing into our town from the magical plane. One glance at Meri, his fur lying flat once more, told me he felt the darkness rapidly recede as well in wake of my spell, the dusty shadows in the shed already lighter for the destruction of the parasitic charm.

Thorn let out a low, appreciative whistle as the last wisps of ivory smoke curled up from the scorched hay. "Remind me not to ever get on your bad side, Kinsey," he remarked in his gravelly voice, a hint of respectful pride warming his tone.

We moved through the fairgrounds with purpose, Thorn leading the way, his face set in a focused mask. The air grew colder as the sun dipped below the horizon, and my senses were on high alert, attuned to any whisper of darkness that might be clinging to the corners of this place. Meri, ever vigilant, stayed right by my side, his gold eyes scanning the shadows.

The first shed we approached was much like Roger's—hay scattered about, tools laid out in anticipation of a competition that now seemed tainted with something sinister. We didn't have to search long before Thorn uncovered another charm, hidden beneath a pile of pumpkin shavings. Its malevolent energy reached out like tendrils of smoke, and I felt it brush against my consciousness, probing for weaknesses to exploit.

Each shed told the same story. Every carver except Jonas and Clara had been targeted by these charms—cursed objects meant to weave despair into the fabric of their beings. The implications churned in my stomach; someone was systematically undermining the competition, using dark magic as their weapon.

"Why would they leave Jonas and Clara out?" Thorn mused aloud as we stood outside Clara's empty shed. "It can't be an oversight."

Meri's tail flicked, a sure sign he was deep in thought—or plotting mischief; with Meri, it was often a toss-up. "Maybe they're involved," he suggested with that typical sarcastic lilt to his voice. "Or maybe our culprit has a soft spot for them."

I considered his words carefully. The absence of the charms in Jonas's and Clara's sheds didn't necessarily implicate them, but it did raise questions—questions that demanded answers we didn't yet have.

Thorn knelt down and examined the floor of Clara's shed, his fingers tracing over grooves in the wood where pumpkin pulp had been scraped away in the frenzy of creation. He stood up, shaking his head. "Nothing here," he confirmed.

I stepped inside the shed after him, letting my magic ripple out subtly in search of any residual traces that might have been left behind by whoever distributed these vile charms. But there was nothing—no echo of dark energy or lingering presence.

We continued our search in silence, methodical and thorough as we inspected Jonas's space next door. It was eerily similar to Clara's: meticulously organized tools, sketches pinned up with care, but no charm to be found.

As we left the last shed behind us, I couldn't shake the feeling that we were missing something. My thoughts swirled with theories and suspicions, each one as elusive as shadows at twilight.

"We need to figure out what connects Jonas and Clara to all this," I said quietly to Thorn as we walked back towards our car parked at the edge of the grounds.

He nodded in agreement, his profile etched against the darkening sky. "We'll get there," he said with confidence that I wished I could fully share.

Meri settled more comfortably into my tote bag, letting out a soft huff. His weight was reassuring.

And so we left the fairgrounds behind us for now— each shed a silent witness to a plan set in motion by an unseen hand—and headed back into Coventry's heart with our minds burdened by questions.

Chapter 10

The drive back from the fairgrounds carried a silence as heavy as the evening fog. Thorn navigated the winding roads, his knuckles white on the steering wheel, eyes narrowed in concentration or maybe contemplation. Beside him, I turned the day's revelations over in my mind, a mental puzzle missing too many crucial pieces.

"It doesn't make sense," I finally broke the silence, voicing the thoughts that had been swirling around in my head. "Why plant those charms in every shed but Jonas's and Clara's? It's too obvious. It's like someone is screaming at us to look at them."

Thorn glanced at me, his profile softened by the dim dashboard lights. "It's either a very clumsy attempt to frame them or a clever ruse to divert our attention. Either way, it points to someone knowing about their connection to Jacob."

I nodded, feeling Meri's steady breathing against my thigh as he snoozed on my lap. His presence was a small comfort amidst the chaos. "And if it's a diversion," I continued, "then our killer is cunning, someone who understands how an investigation works, someone who anticipates our moves."

"We're dealing with someone who knows magic, Kinsley," Thorn said, his voice firm with conviction.

"They know enough to make those charms and to target people sensitive to magic."

I let out a slow breath. "That narrows down our list of suspects significantly. Not many people can wield that kind of dark magic."

Thorn reached over and squeezed my hand.

"The competition," I mused aloud. "Someone wanted to thin out the contestants—give Jonas and Clara a clear shot at winning. Or maybe it was just one of them trying to secure victory."

"Could be," Thorn replied, his tone noncommittal. "But killing for a pumpkin carving competition? That seems extreme."

"People have killed for stranger reasons," I reminded him, thinking of past murders we'd encountered.

Thorn was quiet for a moment before speaking again. "We need to keep an open mind. We can't afford tunnel vision on Jonas and Clara—not when there could be another angle we're missing."

The door closed behind us with a click, sealing away the chill of the evening and the weight of unsolved mysteries. Our home enveloped us in its familiar warmth, the lingering scent of sage from my earlier cleansing ritual a comforting embrace. I moved toward the kitchen, the floorboards creaking underfoot, evidence of the countless footsteps of our family's daily life.

I pulled open the refrigerator, the light spilling out over the tile as I reached for a Coke, its cool aluminum promising a momentary escape. Thorn's preference was more straightforward—a beer.

"I've been thinking," I began, popping the tab on my drink with a satisfying fizz. "Martha Thompson might be our next best lead." I glanced over at Thorn as he twisted off his beer cap, his eyes meeting mine with a readiness that told me he was already steps ahead.

He took a long pull from his bottle before replying. "She's at the center of it all—Jacob's success, Jonas's envy, Clara's ambition. She could give us insight into their dynamics."

I leaned against the counter, sipping my Coke. "She knew Jacob better than anyone," I said. "And she's been hiding her magic from Jonas all these years. Something might have pushed her to do something drastic."

"We'll visit her first thing in the morning," Thorn decided. "We need to understand what really happened between her and Jacob—and how deep Clara and Jonas are in this."

I nodded in agreement, feeling the pieces starting to shift into place within my mind. There was more to uncover—more secrets hidden within the soil of Coventry's pumpkin fields.

With that plan set for morning, we allowed ourselves to retreat from the case for the night, seeking solace in each other's company and in the quiet sanctuary of our home. Tomorrow would come soon enough, bringing with it fresh revelations and truths that could not stay buried forever.

* * *

Water pelted my skin, a comforting cascade that should've washed away the worries of the day before. But instead, grief enveloped me like a shroud, an unexpected deluge of sorrow that had nothing to do with the shower's spray. My breath hitched, sobs racking my body as I leaned against the cool tile. Why was I crying? The sadness was thick, tangible, suffocating.

I turned off the water, urgency cutting through the haze of despair. The grief wasn't mine; it was something else—something external, sinister. I yanked my hair back into a hasty ponytail, droplets flinging from the strands. Pulling on a sweatshirt and sweatpants, I burst from the bathroom.

Meri sat just outside, his eyes flicking up to mine with his usual snark at the ready. "You look like you've been through—"

"Shh." My voice was sharp, silencing him. "Follow me."

We descended the stairs together, Meri's silent presence a comfort despite his earlier teasing. "I'm following a trail of despair," I explained as we reached the bottom step. "It's like tendrils snaking through the house and stabbing me in the heart."

The morning light did nothing to alleviate the shadows that clung to my spirit as we stepped outside. Hangman's tree loomed over us, its branches swaying gently in the breeze. There, among the roots and fallen leaves, were tiny fragments glinting with malevolence.

"Another piece of that damned charm," I muttered.

Meri circled around me, his tail flicking in agitation. "We didn't destroy it completely. Well, let's finish the job."

With focused intent, we set about destroying each sliver of the Misery Curse Charm, their dark power dissipating under our combined efforts. The relief was immediate—a lifting of weight from my chest, a clearing of clouds from my mind.

Breathing easier now that the remnants were gone, I straightened and faced Meri. "Bacon sound good?"

His ears perked up at that, and he trotted toward the house ahead of me. "For once, you're speaking my language."

***

I slid the sizzling bacon from the pan onto a plate, my stomach rumbling in anticipation. Meri paced near my feet, his eyes fixed on the prize. "Patience," I murmured, but he just huffed, his tail twitching with barely contained excitement.

After setting aside a generous portion for Meri, I plated my own breakfast and poured myself a cup of coffee, with sugar and a generous pour of heavy cream. The morning sun filtered through the kitchen window, casting a warm glow on the wooden table where I settled with my laptop. It was time to catch up on the world while I ate.

The aroma of bacon and coffee filled the room as I flipped open my laptop and began scrolling through social media. It was a stream of smiling faces, life updates, and endless ads. A friend from college just got engaged, someone else was on a beach in Mexico... I liked a few posts automatically, my thoughts still partly on the case.

I switched to the news next. Headlines flashed across the screen: politics, environmental concerns, celebrity gossip. I clicked through them methodically until I found something related to pumpkin carving competitions. My heart skipped with hope for a second, but it was just a roundup of events across the country—smiling winners holding giant checks next to their masterpieces. Nothing that could help us understand what happened to Jacob or who's targeting the carvers here in Coventry.

Meri jumped onto the chair beside me and started on his bacon with gusto. "Anything useful?" he asked between bites.

I shook my head. "Just the usual buzz about competitions elsewhere. No leads or anything out of the ordinary."

He paused, licking his lips clean before speaking again. "So we're back to square one?"

"Not exactly." I closed my laptop with a sigh.

Meri finished his breakfast and leaped down from the chair. "Well, when you're ready to go Sherlock Holmes again, you know where to find me."

I chuckled at his comment; even in cat form, his confidence never waned. "Thanks, Meri." Pushing back from the table, I gathered our plates and headed to the sink.

Time ticked by as I washed up, my mind working over everything we knew so far. Thorn was at the station already—he always was an early riser—and he'd expect me mid-morning. That gave me just enough time to get ready and head out.

As much as this case frustrated me with its tangled threads and dead ends, there was something invigorating about it too—the challenge of unraveling a mystery that was more than it seemed. But first things first: I needed another cup of coffee for the road.

***

Martha's garden bloomed with a vibrancy that defied the autumn chill. Her flowers, a riot of color, swayed in the gentle breeze as if dancing to a melody only they could hear. Thorn and I approached along the cobblestone path, our footsteps muffled by the lush grass on either side.

I couldn't help but let my gaze linger on the blossoms, noting the way they seemed to hum with life. It wasn't just the care of a green thumb at work here; there was magic woven into the very soil, a nurturing spell that coaxed each petal and leaf to perfection.

Martha, her hands buried in the dirt of a flowerbed, didn't notice us at first. She wore a wide-brimmed hat that shielded her eyes from the sun, casting her features in shadow. But even from this distance, I could sense her deep connection to the earth she tended.

"Martha," Thorn called out, his voice gentle so as not to startle her.

She looked up then, and a smile spread across her face—a mix of welcome and wariness. "Sheriff Wilson, Kinsley," she greeted us, standing and brushing dirt from her knees. "To what do I owe this visit?"

Thorn glanced at me before taking the lead. "We're just following up on Jacob's case. Mind if we ask you a few questions?"

"Of course not." Martha's voice held a hint of resignation as she gestured for us to follow her to a small wrought-iron table nestled among the flowers.

We took our seats while Martha fetched some iced tea from inside her cozy cottage. The glasses clinked softly as she set them down before us.

I took a sip of the tea, its coolness refreshing against my lips. "Your garden is truly remarkable," I said, allowing my admiration to show.

She smiled faintly. "Thank you. It's my pride and joy."

I leaned forward slightly, choosing my words with care. "The plants seem more than just well-tended. They're thriving in a way that suggests... extra assistance."

Martha met my eyes for a moment before looking away. Her hands fidgeted with her hat brim—a telltale sign of discomfort.

Thorn cleared his throat subtly before speaking. "We're trying to understand more about Jacob's relationship with Clara and Jonas—and yours as well."

Martha sighed, setting down her glass. "I've known them all for years," she began slowly. "Clara's drive to outdo Jacob in carving... it became an obsession."

"And Jonas?" Thorn prompted gently.

"He's always been in Jacob's shadow," Martha said with a hint of sadness. "His bitterness—it affects everything he does."

"Did you ever intervene? With your... gardening abilities?" I asked softly.

Martha hesitated, then nodded reluctantly. "I helped Jacob once after a bad harvest nearly ruined him."

"And Jonas?" I pressed on.

"I've tried to help him too," she admitted. "But he refuses to accept it—doesn't even know his own potential."

Thorn leaned back in his chair, processing this new information while I considered the implications.

Martha's hands hovered protectively over her tea, as if she could shield her thoughts as easily as she could the glass from errant leaves. Thorn leaned forward, elbows resting on the wrought-iron table that seemed too delicate for his solid frame.

"Martha," he said, his voice soft but insistent, "do you have any insights into Clara's state of mind? Any possible motives for her to harm Jacob?"

She shook her head, the brim of her wide hat casting shadows over her eyes. "No, Clara couldn't hurt anyone. She's ambitious, yes, but not violent." Martha paused, her gaze flitting to the vibrant blooms that edged the garden. "But I won't lie—her fixation on surpassing Jacob... it bordered on obsession."

I watched her closely, looking for the flicker of uncertainty or a fleeting shadow of doubt that might suggest she knew more than she was letting on. But Martha's face remained an open book with concern etched into every line.

"Borderline obsession can sometimes push people to extreme actions," I offered cautiously.

Martha's eyes met mine, a glint of steel beneath her outward softness. "Clara wants to be the best; there's no crime in that."

"No," Thorn agreed, "but sometimes the line between ambition and something darker is thinner than we think."

"I saw Essie in Jacob's fields just a couple of days ago," Martha revealed, her voice carrying a hint of accusation. "I confronted her before telling Jacob. She had no business there after leaving the way she did."

I leaned in, my interest piqued. "Essie lived there? On the farm with Jacob?"

Martha nodded, a wistful look crossing her features. "Yes, she was like a daughter to him for a while. But things changed; she left abruptly about a year ago to work for Roger."

"And you're certain Jacob didn't steal Essie's hybrid strain?" I pressed gently, though my gut told me there was more to it.

She met my gaze squarely, her eyes alight with something fierce and protective. "Absolutely. Jacob had his own methods. He didn't need Essie's hybrids."

The conviction in her voice was almost too forceful, too desperate to convince. It struck a chord in me, one that resonated with suspicion. I exchanged a glance with Thorn; he caught it too.

Martha's emphatic denial had the opposite effect on me—it suggested complicity. Had she been the one to help Jacob's pumpkins grow so large? It would explain her defensiveness, her need to steer us away from any thought that Jacob could have appropriated Essie's work.

My mind whirred with possibilities as I considered Martha's potential involvement. The magic in her garden was undeniable; could she have extended that same enchantment to Jacob's pumpkins?

"Martha," I began, my voice even but firm, "you've seen Jacob's pumpkins. They're not just large; they're... extraordinary. Beyond what simple farming can achieve." I watched her closely, saw the flicker of something cross her face—a momentary crack in her composed facade. "Did you help his pumpkins grow using magic?"

Her reaction was immediate and visceral. The color drained from her cheeks as if I'd accused her of witchcraft in a time when such an accusation could mean death. "That's crazy," she sputtered, a touch of indignation coloring her tone. "I'm a gardener, not some... some sorceress."

I leaned back in my chair, the iron framework groaning slightly under the shift in weight. "Martha, we know you have a gift—a talent for making things grow. It's evident in every corner of this place." I gestured broadly at the garden surrounding us.

Thorn chimed in, his voice steady and reassuring. "We're not here to cause trouble for you, Martha. But understanding what happened to Jacob is important. If magic played a part in his success with pumpkins—"

"I've done nothing wrong!" Martha cut him off sharply, her eyes darting from Thorn to me and back again like a trapped animal seeking escape.

"We're not saying you have," I tried to soothe her rising panic. "But if you did help him magically, it might explain some things about his success—and why someone might have resented him enough to..."

Martha pushed herself up from the table with such force that her chair toppled backward onto the grass. Her hands were trembling visibly now, and I felt a pang of guilt for causing her distress.

"I think it's best if you leave," Martha said through clenched teeth, barely managing to keep her composure.

Thorn stood as well, righting Martha's chair with a quiet clatter before placing his sheriff's hat back on his head. "We'll respect your wishes," he said diplomatically.

I stood too but lingered for a moment longer than Thorn, searching Martha's face for any sign of admission or denial that would confirm my suspicions.

"Martha," I said softly, trying one last time to reach out to her, "if there's anything you can tell us—"

"No!" she snapped with finality, cutting me off mid-sentence. "Just go!"

With no other choice but to comply with her request—or more accurately, her demand—I followed Thorn down the path away from Martha's house.

As we reached Thorn's car parked along the curb outside Martha's fence, I paused and glanced back at the cottage nestled amongst the riotous colors of blooms and vines.

"Thorn," I murmured as he opened the driver's side door, "there's more she's not telling us."

He nodded grimly in agreement before sliding into the car. As he started the engine and we pulled away from Martha Thompson's sanctuary of secrets, I couldn't shake the feeling that we had just scratched

the surface of something deeply rooted in magic—
and perhaps in malice as well.

Chapter 11

Thorn maneuvered the cruiser through the maze of country roads leading back to town, his grip on the steering wheel betraying none of the turmoil I felt churning inside me. Martha's garden still lingered in my mind, a vibrant oasis that hummed with more than just the buzz of bees. She had been hiding something; I could feel it in my bones.

"We need to talk to Essie and Clara again," I broke the silence, twisting the silver ring around my finger—a nervous habit. "Their stories are as full of holes as a carved jack-o'-lantern."

Thorn nodded, his jaw tightening as he glanced at me. "Agreed. But we can't split ourselves in two. We should prioritize."

The sun filtered through the cruiser's windshield, casting a warm glow on Thorn's handsome face. "Essie's our best bet first. We know where she should be. Clara might take more finessing."

The festival had come back to life at the fairgrounds, as if Jacob's murder was nothing more than a nightmarish interlude in an otherwise festive autumn tale. I felt a twinge of unease at how quickly people seemed to move on.

Thorn parked near Essie's trailer, the familiar clunk of the gear shift settling like a verdict. We stepped out into the din of laughter and music, a stark contrast to our grim task.

We approached Essie's trailer, and Thorn rapped sharply on the door. Silence greeted us—a silence that hung heavy with implication.

He knocked again, this time adding his authoritative tone. "Essie Elrod, it's Sheriff Wilson. We need to speak with you."

Still no answer.

I leaned close to the window, cupping my hands around my eyes and peering inside. "Nothing," I murmured, stepping back with a frown.

Thorn tested the doorknob; it turned easily in his hand—unlocked. A thread of caution wound its way through my chest as he pushed the door open.

"Essie?" he called out as we entered, announcing our presence into what appeared to be an empty space.

The trailer was as silent as an abandoned crypt, its stillness unsettling against the backdrop of festival noise just outside its thin walls.

Thorn moved ahead of me, his senses honed from years of law enforcement alert for any sign of trouble or foul play.

I followed close behind, my own magic humming beneath my skin—a silent guardian ready at a moment's notice.

We cleared each small room methodically until it was apparent—we were alone in Essie's trailer with no sign of where she might have gone.

I glanced at Thorn, seeing my own concern mirrored in his eyes. "She should have been here," I said quietly.

Thorn and I decided to look around the festival to see if Essie had simply wandered off to partake in the events. Despite the pall cast by Jacob's murder, people were still having fun - eating pumpkin-flavored treats, playing carnival games, and admiring the amateur pumpkin displays. An air of forced levity hung over the grounds, like a brightly colored shroud concealing darker secrets beneath the surface.

We spotted Ted Mellon near the entrance, extolling the virtues of the upcoming professional pumpkin carving competition to any passerby who would listen. I couldn't help but admire his determination to keep the festival running, despite the tragedy that had occurred.

Thorn approached Ted, flashing his badge. "Sheriff Wilson. Got a minute?"

Ted turned, his broad smile faltering only slightly at the sight of Thorn's uniform. "Of course, of course! What can I do for Coventry's finest?" His booming voice carried across the fairgrounds.

Thorn's voice dropped to a more discreet volume. "We were just wondering if you're still planning on hosting the carving competition? Even with..." he hesitated, "...the situation with Jacob?"

Ted nodded vigorously, puffing out his chest. "Absolutely! HappyTummy Organic Farms is fully committed to seeing this festival through. It's what Jacob would have wanted." He shook his head, looking properly mournful for a moment before his upbeat demeanor returned. "The show must go on, as they say!"

I studied Ted curiously, wondering if his persistence had more to do with profits and corporate sponsorships than honoring Jacob's memory. "What if you lose more competitors?" I asked. "Roger Harris was just hospitalized. Will you still host the event if you're down to only one or two carvers?"

At this, Ted's facade cracked ever so slightly, his eyes darting away nervously. "Well, ah, contractually we need at least two participants for the televised competition." He leaned in, dropping his voice. "But between you and me, as long as we have Jonas Thompson, we're good. He's the fan favorite now, being local and all. The cameras will be on him."

Ted glanced around surreptitiously before continuing. "Don't repeat this, but frankly, it would be ideal if Roger dropped out too. More attention on Jonas that way." He flashed his salesman's grin, though it didn't reach his eyes.

I frowned, displeased with his callous attitude. But it wasn't unexpected. Ted likely cared more about profits than people. We left him to his promotional antics, continuing our search for Essie with troubled minds.

As Thorn and I meandered through the festival crowd, I couldn't shake the uneasy feeling crawling up my spine. Essie's absence from her trailer, Ted's cavalier attitude towards the competition despite the dark cloud of Jacob's death—it all gnawed at me, leaving a sour taste in my mouth. The tang of fried dough and the scent of pumpkin spice did little to sweeten my disposition.

Then, out of the corner of my eye, I caught a flicker of movement—a shadow that seemed out of place among the revelers. I turned sharply, and there she was—Lisa, skulking near a row of porta-potties like a cat on the prowl. My heart hammered against my ribs, a primal warning signal that blared through my senses.

"Thorn," I said softly, touching his arm to get his attention. "I need to use the restroom. I'll be right back."

He glanced over at me, concern etched on his face. "Do you want me to walk over there with you?"

I shook my head no, forcing a smile. "I'll be fine. Keep an eye out for Essie; I won't be long."

As he turned back toward the crowd, I made a beeline for the porta-potties, slipping behind one instead of going inside. The din of festivalgoers faded into a muted buzz as I crouched down and waited. The sharp smell of disinfectant stung my nostrils.

Minutes ticked by like hours as I held my breath, listening for any sign of Lisa's approach. Then there it was—the crunch of gravel underfoot growing closer and closer until it stopped just on the other side of my hiding spot.

"Kinsley?" Lisa's voice was tinged with mock concern. "Are you in there? We need to talk."

My blood simmered with anger as I stepped out from behind the porta-potty and faced her. "Talk? Is that what you call stalking me and my family?"

Lisa's eyes widened in feigned innocence before narrowing into slits. "Oh, please," she scoffed, "like you're so innocent yourself. But it doesn't matter; soon enough, Thorn will realize he's better off with me."

My jaw clenched so tight it hurt. This woman threatened everything I held dear—my husband, my children, our life together. She had no idea who she was dealing with.

"You listen to me," I hissed through gritted teeth, "you will stay away from Thorn and my family or so help me—"

"Or what?" Lisa taunted, stepping closer into my space with a smirk playing on her lips.

The air around us crackled with energy as my temper flared out of control. My hand lifted involuntarily as if pulled by an unseen force, palm facing Lisa.

"I'll make you disappear," I spat out each word like venom. My hand began to glow with an ethereal light—magic imbued with ancient power that pulsed through my veins.

Lisa's smirk faltered as she took in the display before her eyes—a visible threat manifesting in ways she couldn't understand or anticipate.

"I'm not someone you want to mess with," I continued, the light from my hand casting eerie shadows across both our faces. "And if you push me any further—if you dare threaten my family again—I won't hold back."

Fear flashed in Lisa's eyes for just a moment before she masked it with defiance once more. She took a step back but didn't turn away completely.

"This isn't over," she spat out before turning on her heel and storming off into the crowd.

I watched her go until she was swallowed up by the sea of people enjoying their pumpkin-spiced festivities, oblivious to the dark undercurrents swirling around them.

Lowering my hand, I felt the magic recede back into myself like a wave pulling away from the shore. A shudder ran through me at how close I'd come to unleashing it fully upon Lisa—an act that would have had consequences far beyond our personal feud.

Taking a deep breath to steady myself, I walked back towards Thorn, who was waiting near a stand selling hot cider. His brow furrowed in concern as he saw me approach.

"Everything all right?" he asked immediately.

I let out a weary sigh as I reached Thorn's side. "I had a run-in with Lisa just now," I confessed, watching his expression morph from concern to anger.

"What?" He glanced around sharply as if expecting to spot her lurking nearby. "Why didn't you come get me? You shouldn't have confronted her alone."

I lifted a hand to gently touch his arm. "It's okay. I didn't seek her out; she cornered me while I was waiting for you. But I handled it."

Thorn's jaw clenched, his protective instincts on high alert. "Still, she's clearly unstable. Who knows what she's capable of?"

"She's capable of being a nuisance, nothing more," I said firmly. "I know you're worried, but one mortal woman is no match for me."

I held his gaze, allowing a hint of magic to swirl in my eyes—a subtle reminder of the power I wielded, even if I chose not to use it frivolously.

Thorn's shoulders relaxed a fraction as understanding dawned on him. Of course I could protect myself against the likes of Lisa with barely an effort. He was letting his emotions cloud his judgment.

"You're right," he conceded. "I just hate feeling powerless to shield you and the girls from her harassment."

I softened my tone, touched by his devotion. "I know. But you have to trust me to handle things on the magical front. Lisa should be the one afraid, not us."

Thorn nodded, the crease between his brows easing. "Okay. I'll try to rein in the overprotective urges. But promise you'll tell me if she escalates things further?"

"I promise," I assured him. "For now, let's focus on finding Essie. I have a bad feeling about her disappearance."

Chapter 12

As Thorn and I threaded through the festival crowd, the mingled scents of cinnamon and sugar seemed to sweeten the chill in the air. I clutched my sweater closer, eyes scanning for a glimpse of fiery red or that distinctive bitter edge that marked Essie's presence. A flicker of movement near one of the food trucks caught my attention. A figure hunched over a steaming cup, unmistakable auburn locks tumbling over hunched shoulders.

"There," I murmured, nudging Thorn's arm. "By the truck serving cider."

We moved closer, our approach unnoticed by Essie as she blew gently on her drink. I cleared my throat. "Essie?"

She jerked upright, spilling some of her cider. Eyes narrowed as she took us in, a defensive shield instantly up. "Sheriff Wilson, Kinsley. What do you want now?"

"We're just tying up some loose ends," Thorn said, his voice even but firm. "Mind if we chat?"

She sighed and set her cup down on the counter behind her. "I suppose you won't leave me alone until we do."

We stepped aside from the bustle, finding a semblance of privacy beside a stack of hay bales.

"I know you've been in Jacob's pumpkin patch recently," I began, watching her closely for any telltale reaction.

Essie's lips tightened into a thin line. "So what if I was? That land used to be as much mine as his."

"Did you take anything from there?" Thorn asked.

Her gaze flitted away for a moment before meeting mine again with unflinching resolve. "I took samples of his plant," she admitted with a slight edge to her voice. "I needed proof that he stole my hybrid strain."

"And did you find what you were looking for?" My curiosity piqued; after all, Jacob had sworn those pumpkins were all his doing.

A shadow crossed Essie's face, an interplay of anger and vindication. "Yes, I found it," she said with bitter triumph. "It was unmistakable—my strain's unique vine pattern was all over his patch."

Thorn shifted beside me, his lawman's instinct kicking in. "Essie, did you confront Jacob about this?"

"I didn't get the chance to." She shrugged with a hint of frustration coloring her tone. "But don't think for a second that I'm sad he's gone."

"But you didn't do anything to him that day? You weren't caught on his land?" Thorn pressed on, trying to peel back layers to find some semblance of truth.

Essie shook her head emphatically. "No, nothing like that." Her voice carried the ring of honesty—or at least she believed it to be so.

I watched her face closely—every twitch and every glance—searching for the slip or sign that would betray more than she wanted to share. But there was none, only the same stony resolve that had met us since we arrived.

I studied Essie carefully, sensing there was more she wasn't telling us. Her body language was defensive, arms crossed tightly across her chest as if barricading herself against revealing anything further. She leaned away from us slightly, angling her body towards the door.

"Essie," I said gently, "is there anything else you can share with us about that day? Even the smallest detail could help."

She hesitated, eyes flickering between Thorn and me. I could see the internal debate raging behind them as she weighed her options. She bit her lip, conflicted. I decided to press just a little more to see if she would open up.

"We know you and Jacob had your differences in the past," I continued. "But someone killed him in cold blood. Don't you want to see justice done for him?"

Essie let out a heavy sigh, shoulders slumping in resignation as she realized she had little choice but to cooperate. "There is one thing," she admitted slowly. "When I was leaving his property that day, I heard raised voices coming from the big red barn near the back of the land."

Thorn and I exchanged a meaningful glance. This could be exactly the lead we needed.

"I recognized Jacob's voice right away. He sounded angry, which wasn't unusual for his temperament." Essie shook her head, lips pressed in a thin line. "But the woman's voice...that surprised me. It was Martha Thompson."

My brow furrowed in confusion as I tried to make sense of this new information. What business could Martha have had with Jacob to elicit such anger from him?

"I didn't catch everything they said." Essie bit her lip anxiously. "But I heard Martha say something about them needing to start acting like brothers. And Jacob shouted at her to get off his land immediately and never come back."

Brothers? Jonas and Jacob were about the same age and had no familial connection that I knew of. I struggled to make sense of it all.

"Did you hear anything else?" I asked. "Even if it seemed insignificant at the time, it could be helpful."

Essie's gaze shifted past us, landing on something in the distance that only she could see. "There's one more thing," she said, voice dropping as if the words were reluctant to come out. "Before Ted called us all together for the intro ceremony, I saw Clara."

My interest piqued at the mention of Clara's name. The woman's obsession with Jacob had already painted her in shades of gray in my mind. "What about Clara?" I prompted.

Essie glanced around as if to make sure no one was eavesdropping on our conversation, even though we were well out of earshot from the nearest festival-goer. "She has a shed here, like the rest of us," Essie continued, "but I caught her sneaking out of what looked like Jacob's shed. It was odd, you know? She was acting all sneaky."

Thorn raised an eyebrow. "Are you sure it was Jacob's shed and not her own?"

Essie frowned, biting her lip as she considered. "I can't say for certain," she admitted with a reluctant shrug. "But Clara looked... guilty, if you know what I mean. Like she didn't want to be seen."

I could feel the wheels turning in Thorn's head as he processed this new information. He took out his notepad and jotted down a few quick notes before tucking it away again.

"Anything else?" Thorn asked, his tone gentle yet probing.

"No, that's it," Essie replied with a definitive nod. She seemed eager to be done with our questioning, her eyes darting to the exit more than once.

"Thank you, Essie," I said, giving her a small smile that I hoped conveyed both gratitude and reassurance. "You've been very helpful."

She offered us a curt nod before excusing herself, retreating quickly back into the crowd and leaving Thorn and me to digest this latest tidbit.

Chapter 13

I rubbed my temples, the residue of magic and mystery from the day weighing heavy on my mind. Thorn sat across from me in the cruiser, his brows furrowed as he mulled over Essie's revelations. The silence between us buzzed with unspoken theories.

"Martha might be more involved than we thought," I ventured, breaking the stillness. "If she's using magic on those pumpkins and possibly Jacob's mother..."

Thorn nodded, his jaw setting in that determined way that meant he was piecing together a puzzle only he could see. "And if she's been keeping this a secret all along, there's no telling what else she might be hiding."

The idea of Martha, gentle and nurturing with her plants, being at the center of this dark web didn't sit right with me. Yet, the facts were stacking up like tarot cards foretelling a grim future.

"We need to push her on it," Thorn said decisively.

My gut clenched at the thought of confronting Martha again. The woman had always been kind to me, sharing herb cuttings and gardening tips. But kindness could be a veneer, and underneath it could lie secrets dark enough to kill for.

"Let's do it," I agreed. "We can't let personal feelings get in the way."

Thorn put the cruiser into gear and we headed back to Martha's house. The drive was short but filled with an anticipatory tension that buzzed through my veins like a current.

When we arrived, I noticed immediately how the garden seemed to welcome us, flowers nodding in the breeze as if they recognized friends. But there was an undercurrent there too—a whisper of magic that raised goosebumps on my arms.

We found Martha farther back in her garden, her hands buried deep in the rich soil as she tended to her plants with an almost maternal affection. She didn't seem surprised to see us, but her welcome was as brittle as the dried leaves that crunched under our feet.

"Martha," Thorn greeted her, his voice carrying a gentle firmness that demanded attention. "We need to talk."

She straightened up slowly, brushing dirt from her hands onto her apron. Her eyes darted between us, a flicker of something unreadable passing over her features. "I've already told you everything I know," she said, though her voice lacked conviction.

I stepped closer, my own magic humming softly beneath my skin in response to the latent energy that enveloped her garden. "Martha, we're not here to accuse you," I said softly, trying to coax out the truth with kindness rather than force. "But there are things that don't add up, and we think you can help us understand."

Her gaze lingered on me for a moment longer than necessary, and I saw a hint of sorrow in those deep-set eyes. She was holding back—of that I was certain.

Thorn cleared his throat, drawing Martha's attention back to him. "We can have this conversation here or down at the station," he suggested, his tone even but leaving no room for argument.

The threat hung in the air between us like a heavy perfume, overly sweet and suffocating. Martha glanced at her beloved plants before nodding stiffly. "Let's talk here," she conceded with a sigh that seemed to carry the weight of years upon it.

"Martha," Thorn began, his voice calm but carrying an undercurrent of urgency, "We talked to Essie Elrod, and she mentioned something about a conversation she overheard. Something that suggested Jacob and Jonas might be more than just neighbors or competitors."

Martha's hands balled into fists, and she looked up at us. Her face was a mask of composure, but her eyes betrayed a flicker of unease. She took a deep breath, as if she were about to dive into waters too deep and too dark.

"I don't know what Essie thinks she heard," she started, her voice steady but tinged with something that sounded like fear.

"Martha," I interjected gently, "if there's something you need to get off your chest, now's the time. It could help us understand what happened to Jacob."

She glanced at me then, and I could see the walls crumbling behind her eyes. There was a story there, one that had been locked away for far too long.

"It's true," she whispered after a moment that stretched between us like the last thread of hope before it snaps. "Jonas is Jacob's half-brother."

The words hung in the air, laden with years of hidden pain and secret bonds. I felt Thorn stiffen beside me, even he hadn't been prepared for this.

"How?" he asked, his voice betraying none of the shock that must have been coursing through him.

Martha sank onto a stone bench nestled among her flowers. She seemed smaller somehow, diminished by the weight of her confession.

"Many years ago," she began, her gaze distant as if she were watching the past unfold before her eyes once more, "I had an affair with Jacob's father. It was a terrible mistake—one born out of loneliness and longing—and it resulted in Jonas."

She paused, collecting herself before continuing. "Henrietta—Jacob's adopted mother—was my best friend. What I did... it was unforgivable." The regret in her voice was palpable; it seeped into the very air around us. "The fact that Henrietta adopted Jacob and raised him as her own after her husband betrayed her, well, it says a lot about how good she is."

"And Jacob?" Thorn pressed gently.

Martha looked up at him then, her eyes shining with unshed tears. "I cared for him because he was an innocent in all this mess. And, yes," she admitted, "I felt guilty for betraying Henrietta."

Thorn nodded slowly as if each nod helped him piece together the fragmented image of a family torn apart by secrets and lies.

"Did Jonas know?" I asked quietly.

"Jonas noticed," Martha said, her voice barely above a murmur. "He saw how I would look at Jacob, the care I gave him, and he resented it. Jonas was never easy; he was a stormy child, full of sharp edges and dark moods. But he was my son, and I loved him fiercely."

I could hear in her tone the love of a mother for her child—a love that could smother as surely as it could support. She clasped her hands together, knuckles white with the effort of holding herself together.

"As he grew up, Jonas's resentment toward Jacob festered," she continued. "He believed Jacob had everything—talent, charm, success—and he hated him for it."

Thorn shifted beside me, his gaze never leaving Martha's face. "So you became overprotective of Jonas," he prompted gently.

Martha nodded, a lock of hair falling across her face. She brushed it away impatiently. "Yes," she admitted. "I suppose I did. It wasn't fair to either of them— Jacob or Jonas—but I couldn't help it. All I wanted was for Jonas to be happy."

I felt a pang of sympathy for Martha, caught between two sons—one she had raised and the other she'd given away. It was a no-win situation, and now people were paying the price for that long-ago decision.

"The argument Essie heard..." Thorn's voice trailed off as he encouraged Martha to fill in the blanks.

Martha looked up at us with eyes that had seen too much and held too much back. "That argument," she said slowly, "was me telling Jacob the truth." She paused as if reliving that moment all over again. "I asked him to please withdraw from the carving competition so Jonas could have a win. Just one win."

I could imagine how that conversation must have gone—Martha pleading with one son for her other son's happiness while Jacob stood there, probably shocked by the revelation and the request being made of him.

"Jacob refused," Martha whispered, and there was a crack in her voice that spoke volumes. "He told me he hated me and didn't want to be Jonas's brother."

The words hung heavy in the air between us like ripe fruit ready to drop. The pain in Martha's confession twisted something inside me—a reminder that secrets have a way of growing beyond our control until they strangle everything around them.

I looked at Thorn, saw my own horror reflected in his eyes. How do you reconcile with knowing your whole life is built on a lie?

The breeze picked up then, rustling through the leaves with a mournful sound that seemed to echo Martha's sorrow. I stepped closer to her, reaching out to offer what comfort I could.

"Martha," I said softly, trying to bridge the gap between us with my words. "You've been carrying this alone for too long."

She reached out then and grasped my hand like a lifeline, her grip surprisingly strong despite her earlier frailty.

"I thought if Jacob stepped aside just once," she said through tears that finally began to fall freely, "Jonas would see his own worth."

"And now Jacob is dead," Thorn said quietly but not unkindly. "I have to ask… did you have anything to do with that?"

Martha's tears, each a crystalline drop of regret, traced lines down her weathered cheeks as she spoke.

"I could never harm Jacob," she insisted, her voice shaking with emotion. "Despite everything, I loved him. You must believe me."

I did believe her. The pain etched into her face was not the kind that could be feigned or fabricated. It was raw and real, the kind that comes from love tangled with grief.

"But Jonas…" Thorn prodded gently, always the sheriff even in moments as fragile as this.

Martha drew in a shuddering breath and wiped at her eyes with the back of her hand. "Jonas doesn't know about Jacob being his half-brother," she confessed. "I saw him struggling with his anger, and it was poisoning everything around him, especially his crops. I just wanted them to bridge the gap before it was too late."

"Did you ever tell Jonas how his negativity was affecting his harvest?" I asked, kneeling beside her on the soft earth.

Martha shook her head, a fresh wave of tears spilling over. "I couldn't," she whispered. "How do you tell your son that his heart is so full of bitterness it's rotting away everything he touches?"

Her words hung heavy between us. I could see Thorn's jaw clench as he processed what this meant for our investigation.

"We need to talk to Jonas again," Thorn said after a moment of heavy silence.

Martha nodded slowly, resigned. "Yes, you do," she agreed. "But please be gentle with him. He's been through so much already."

Standing up, I offered Martha my hand and helped her to her feet. "We'll do our best," I assured her, though I knew that some truths cut too deep to handle with anything resembling gentleness.

As we left Martha's garden behind us, I couldn't help but glance back at the plants swaying in the gentle breeze—so alive and vibrant despite the shadow of death that loomed over them.

In the cruiser on our way back to town, Thorn's fingers tapped an impatient rhythm on the steering wheel—a sign he was deep in thought.

"Do you think Jonas could have found out about Jacob and lashed out?" I asked, breaking the silence.

Thorn shrugged slightly, his gaze fixed on the road ahead. "It's possible," he admitted. "If he discovered their connection on his own... It might explain a lot."

Chapter 14

"You okay?" Thorn asked.

"Yeah," I replied, taking a deep breath. "Just... a lot to process."

He nodded. "Martha's story changes things," he said, drumming his fingers on the steering wheel. "What about Clara? If Clara found out about Jonas being Jacob's half-brother..."

I finished his thought. "It could have pushed her over the edge. Jealousy can be a powerful motivator, especially mixed with love." My mind raced with the possibilities. Clara's obsession with surpassing Jacob, her relationship with Jonas—it was a volatile combination.

"And Essie saw Clara sneaking around near Jacob's shed," Thorn added.

I frowned, recalling Essie's words and the uncertainty in them. "She wasn't sure it was Jacob's shed. But it's a lead worth following."

We headed toward the station in silence. As we drove, I couldn't shake the image of Clara Greenway—her eyes filled with that mix of admiration and envy as she stared at Jacob's work at the festival. Her passion for pumpkin carving was undeniable, but was it enough to drive her to murder?

"Jealousy," I mused aloud. "Jealousy over talent, and now possibly jealousy over familial bonds she may have wanted exclusively for herself and Jonas."

Thorn glanced at me briefly before focusing back on the road. "Could be she thought eliminating Jacob would solve all her problems."

"Or," I continued, my voice tinged with doubt, "it could be someone is setting Clara up to take the fall."

We pulled into the station parking lot and sat there for a moment before getting out. Thorn rested his hand on mine, and then we went inside.

In his office, we laid out all we knew on a whiteboard—the relationships, the motives, and our alibis for everyone involved.

"So if Clara knew about Jonas and Jacob," Thorn said as he wrote 'Sibling Rivalry?' in bold letters on the board, "that could have been enough to tip her over."

I leaned against his desk, crossing my arms as I considered it all. "We need more evidence," I stated firmly. "Something that ties her directly to Jacob's murder."

"Agreed." He paused, looking at me with concern etched into his features. "But, Kinsley... if we're going down this path with Clara—"

"We have to be certain before we accuse her of anything." I cut him off.

Thorn nodded gravely. "We should go talk to her."

We headed to Clara's home, a heavy quiet laden with the burden of unresolved issues filling the space between us. The little house sat nestled among tall oaks, its windows dark and unwelcoming. We parked across the street, our eyes fixed on the quiet facade.

We walked up to the front door, and Thorn did his "it's the police" knock. After a few minutes, it became obvious nobody was going to answer the door. I strolled down the driveway and looked into her garage window. No car. It appeared Clara wasn't home.

As I walked back to the front of the house, I saw that Thorn was already on the phone, his voice low but firm as he spoke to the judge. I knew he was doing everything by the book, securing a warrant before we could even think of stepping foot inside Clara's home. It was too bad he was with me, because I would have popped the lock and gone in... had I been alone.

As he hung up, he caught my gaze and gave a small nod. "Warrant's on its way," he said.

"Good." I watched the house, imagining all the possible evidence hidden behind those walls that could lead us to Jacob's killer.

While we waited, Thorn turned to me, his expression serious. "About Lisa," he started, his brow furrowed with concern.

I shifted in my seat to face him. "I can handle Lisa," I assured him.

"I know you can," he said quickly. "But I don't want you confronting her alone again."

I sighed. Thorn's protective nature was both endearing and frustrating at times. "She's not going to stop, Thorn. She's made that clear."

His hand found mine, his grip firm and reassuring. "I get it, Kinsley. But promise me—next time you'll have me with you. We'll work together to arrest her. I want to handle all of this through the justice system. I want her locked away."

Looking into his earnest blue eyes, I saw the worry lurking there—the fear of losing me to some madwoman's vendetta. I nodded slowly. "All right, Thorn. I promise." But my mind drifted to the jars on my mantle... she could go in one of those. Or the family crypt... that would certainly hold her...

A squad car pulled up behind us, and an officer stepped out with paperwork in hand—the warrant.

"Showtime," Thorn murmured as we stepped out of the cruiser.

With the warrant clutched in Thorn's hand, we approached Clara's garage. The overhead door yawned open as I pushed it up, revealing a space that doubled as a workshop. Even without crossing the threshold, my eyes were drawn to an array of pumpkin carvings that cluttered the benches and spilled onto the floor. Each one was more elaborate than the last, but it wasn't their artistry that captured my attention—it was their subject matter.

Violence seethed from every carving. One depicted a scene straight from a horror film, another showed an intricate dance of predators and prey, teeth bared and claws outstretched. But it was the carving sitting alone on the central workbench that sent a shiver down my spine. It was unmistakably a recreation of Jacob's murder scene.

I exchanged a glance with Thorn. "Looks like we've got more than just pumpkins here," he said, stepping inside for a closer look. I followed, drawn in despite myself.

The pumpkins were masterfully done, but each stroke of the knife seemed fueled by something dark and frenetic. I circled the carving of Jacob's death—a blow to the head, surrounded by half-finished pumpkins—just as we'd found him. My gaze lingered on the detail, the way the knife had been wielded with both precision and fury.

"This is... intense," I said finally, searching for the right word.

"Obsessive," Thorn corrected quietly, his eyes scanning the room for additional clues.

"Could she have been practicing?" I wondered aloud. "Rehearsing for what she planned to do to Jacob?"

"Possibly," Thorn replied. "Or working through some twisted fantasy." He snapped photos of each carving with his phone, documenting everything before we moved anything.

We sifted through her tools—knives of every size and shape lay meticulously arranged on magnetic strips along one wall. On her desk, sketches and blueprints were strewn around, designs for carvings that ranged from the grotesque to the ghoulish.

I paused at one sketch in particular. It wasn't violent like the others; it was different—sorrowful almost—a figure hunched over in defeat or despair. It didn't fit with Clara's other work.

"Thorn," I called him over, pointing to the drawing.

He studied it for a moment before nodding slowly. "It's out of place," he agreed.

I felt a nagging pull at my senses—the intuition that there was more here than met the eye. I reached out with my magic subtly, feeling for any trace of dark energy or enchantment. There was nothing overtly magical about Clara's work—just passion turned sour.

I moved on to a shelf crammed with volumes on pumpkin carving techniques, competitive strategies, and... one book stood out: 'The Psychology of Competition.' I pulled it from its place and flipped through its pages until I stumbled upon several passages underlined in red:

"Jealousy can drive individuals to extreme behaviors..."

"Obsession can cloud judgment and warp perception..."

"The need to win can become all-consuming..."

It read like a map to Clara's mindset—each underlined sentence resonated with what we knew about her relationship with Jacob and Jonas.

"We need to find out if she knew about Jonas being Jacob's half-brother," I said as I placed the book back on its shelf.

Thorn nodded as he pocketed his phone. "That could be our missing link."

Thorn was searching the rest of the garage shelves and came across a cardboard box. He pulled it out into the light, and I leaned in to see what he'd uncovered. The contents were innocuous at first glance—newspaper clippings, a scattering of notebooks—but the details within painted a vivid picture of obsession.

He flipped through the clippings, each one meticulously snipped from various publications, all focusing on Jacob's triumphs in pumpkin carving. My eyes darted over the headlines: "Local Artist Takes Top Prize," "Appleton Farms' Pumpkins Unbeatable," "Master Carver Jacob Appleton Does It Again." There was even a photo of Jacob, beaming with a ribbon-adorned pumpkin at his side. The sight twisted my stomach—not out of jealousy, but concern for how deep Clara's obsession might have run.

Thorn's hand moved to the notebooks. They were filled with notes in Clara's tight scrawl, annotations about Jacob's carving techniques. He held one up for me to see, and I skimmed the page. It was more than just notes—it was analysis, speculation, almost as if she was trying to crawl inside Jacob's mind and understand how he worked.

"I knew she was dedicated to her craft," I said slowly, "but this is something else."

Thorn nodded grimly. "Hours upon hours watching his YouTube tutorials and competitions." He tapped a finger against one of the pages where Clara had paused a video frame by frame to describe every detail of Jacob's hand movements.

I felt a chill as I realized that each page was a window into Clara's psyche—a mind so consumed by the need to best Jacob that it could very well have driven her to do the unthinkable.

"We need to talk to her again," Thorn said with conviction. "She has some explaining to do."

I agreed but couldn't shake a sliver of doubt. Obsession didn't always equate to murder. And yet, everything here screamed that Clara wanted nothing more than to dethrone Jacob as Coventry's pumpkin carving king.

I looked back at the box and its unsettling contents. What if it wasn't just about surpassing him? What if it was personal? If Clara had discovered the secret of Jonas and Jacob's kinship, what then? The motive would certainly be there: eliminating Jacob not just for fame but for love.

"Let's see if there are any more clues here," Thorn suggested, pulling out another notebook.

We sifted through pages upon pages of observations and strategies that Clara had jotted down during her intense study sessions of Jacob's work. Some entries were analytical, others veered into rants about how she could do better if only given the chance.

It wasn't long before Thorn uncovered something else—a journal hidden among the notebooks. He opened it carefully, revealing entries that delved deeper into Clara's emotional state than mere notes ever could.

The journal was like stepping directly into Clara's mind—each entry more revealing than the last. Her words vacillated between reverence for Jacob's talent and a bitter loathing for his success over hers. I couldn't help but wince at passages where she described herself as 'living in his shadow,' despite her efforts to shine.

One entry in particular caught my eye—an outpouring of frustration after a competition where Jacob took first place yet again:

"His pumpkins mock me with their perfection... but no more. I will not be second best—not when I know I am better."

I looked up at Thorn with concern creasing my brow. "This is more than just admiration turned sour."

He nodded solemnly before continuing his examination of the box's contents.

There were diagrams as well—sketches where Clara had tried to replicate or even improve upon Jacob's designs. Next to each attempt were annotations critiquing her own work harshly when compared to his.

And then there was an entry dated just days before the competition:

"The festival is coming up... It's now or never. I will show them all."

It wasn't explicit—it didn't say 'I'm going to kill Jacob'—but it didn't need to be. The subtext was clear enough when paired with everything else we'd found.

Chapter 15

Thorn and I were about to enter Clara's house to continue our search when her little red sedan came barreling down the street. She screeched to a halt in the driveway when she saw us standing on her porch. For a moment, we all just stared at each other in surprise. Then Clara's eyes narrowed, and before I could even react, she threw the car into reverse and stomped on the gas pedal.

The tires squealed as the car shot backwards down the driveway. Clara spun the wheel, sending the sedan fishtailing as she changed direction. The engine roared as she slammed it into drive and tore off down the road, leaving a cloud of dust in her wake.

"Well, that wasn't at all suspicious," Meri drawled as he sauntered up next to me, his tail swishing lazily. "I can't imagine why she'd run at the sight of the sheriff rifling through her things."

I shot him an annoyed look, but he just blinked innocently up at me. Meanwhile, Thorn was already on the radio calling for backup.

"Jeremy, Clara Greenway just spotted me and Kinsley at her house and fled the scene at high speed in a red sedan, license plate Charlie-Alpha-Romeo-Six-Nine-Five. I'm in pursuit, request intercept if you can get ahead of her."

He clicked off the radio and turned to me, his expression tense. "I want you to stay here, Kinsley. I don't want you getting hurt if she decides to do something desperate."

I started to protest, but he cut me off. "Please, just this once, listen to me. I can't worry about you and focus on catching her at the same time."

I pressed my lips together unhappily. I didn't like being sidelined, but he had a point. "Fine. But you be careful too."

He gave me a quick kiss. "Always am. We'll finish searching the house when I bring her in." Then he jumped in the cruiser and took off after Clara, lights flashing.

I watched until the flashing lights disappeared around a corner. Beside me, Meri made a thoughtful noise. "Don't know about you, but I could use a pick-me-up after that fun encounter." He looked up at me expectantly.

"We're not leaving to get food right now," I admonished.

"Well, there might be something in the house."

"We're not stealing food from her house, Meri."

"Wouldn't hurt to just go in and take a look around…" he groused.

"All right, we're here to investigate, not stand around. Let's see what Clara was so eager to hide." Meri padded beside me as I pushed open the door and stepped into Clara's home.

The interior was meticulous—every item in its place, every surface polished. I couldn't help but admire the dedication it must take to maintain such order. "Looks like she keeps everything else in her life as controlled as her art," I murmured.

Meri sniffed disdainfully at a porcelain cat figurine perched on a shelf. "Or she's good at hiding the chaos just beneath the surface."

I wandered through the living room, eyes scanning for anything out of place. But nothing seemed amiss—no stray papers, no hidden notes. It was almost too perfect.

Entering the kitchen, I noticed a stack of mail on the counter. Bills, flyers, a few letters—nothing unusual until I spotted an envelope with Jacob's name on it. My heart quickened. "Meri, look at this."

He hopped onto the counter, his eyes narrowing as he peered at the envelope. "Well, that's interesting."

I slid a finger under the flap and pulled out a letter. It was from Jacob to Clara, full of praise for her talent and encouragement for her career. It seemed genuine and kind—a huge contrast to Clara's obsessive behavior.

"Doesn't look like he saw her as a threat," I said softly.

"Maybe not to his career," Meri agreed. "But perhaps to something else?"

I was about to respond when a sudden wave of anxiety crashed over me. Thorn should have been back by now, shouldn't he? He was just going after Clara; it wasn't supposed to be dangerous.

My hands trembled as I set down the letter, my mind racing with horrific possibilities. What if Clara had a gun? What if she crashed into him? The silence of the house pressed in on me, suffocating.

"Thorn…" The word escaped me as a whisper, choked by fear.

Meri jumped down from the counter and rubbed against my leg. "Hey, Kinsley," he said softly, his usual sarcasm gone. "He'll be back."

But his reassurance did nothing to ease the dread coiling in my stomach. I could feel it—the certainty that something had happened to Thorn, that he wasn't coming back and my world was falling apart.

The house felt suddenly claustrophobic, filled with shadows even though sunlight streamed through the windows. I needed air; I needed to move or scream or do something other than stand there waiting for news that might never come.

Meri seemed affected too; his ears were flat against his head, and his tail drooped low. He padded closer and leaned into me more firmly.

I knelt down beside him and wrapped my arms around his large form, burying my face in his fur. He didn't protest or make any of his usual quips; instead, he simply stayed still and let me hold him.

"We're okay," he said quietly after a moment. "We're both okay."

But it felt like a lie because nothing would ever be okay again if Thorn...

I shook my head fiercely, trying to dispel the thoughts threatening to overwhelm me.

"We need to keep looking," I told Meri as I stood up shakily, but I was on the verge of curling into a ball and bawling my eyes out.

My head pounded with a dull ache, my thoughts swirling in a vortex of fear and anxiety. I couldn't shake the feeling that something terrible had happened to Thorn. The more I tried to focus on searching Clara's house, the more the darkness seemed to close in on me.

"It's happening again, isn't it?" I muttered, barely recognizing my own voice as it trembled with the weight of despair.

Meri's eyes met mine, a flicker of concern within their depths. "The charm," he confirmed. "There must be one here somewhere."

I forced myself to take deep breaths, fighting the oppressive sensation. I couldn't afford to lose myself to this feeling—not now. "We have to find it," I said with determination I didn't feel.

Together, we scoured Clara's living room once more, looking under furniture and cushions, checking behind paintings and within decorative vases. Yet no matter where we searched, the charm remained elusive.

Meri leapt onto a bookshelf, his nose twitching as he sniffed at the spines of neatly arranged books. "Nothing," he growled in frustration. "It's like searching for a needle in a haystack—if the needle wanted to stay hidden."

My gaze swept over Clara's pristine kitchen again, but this time it was through a haze of hopelessness that clouded my vision. It felt as though my limbs were weighed down by lead, every movement an effort.

"Kinsley," Meri said softly, his tail flicking with agitation. "We need to step outside."

I nodded numbly and followed him to the door. The moment we stepped out of Clara's house and into the bright sunlight of the afternoon, it was like emerging from underwater—the pressure lifted slightly from my chest, allowing me to draw a fuller breath.

The charm's influence lessened with each step we took away from the house, but it clung stubbornly to the edges of my mind like cobwebs I couldn't brush away.

I sat down on a nearby bench, trying to shake off the remnants of desolation that clung stubbornly to my soul. Meri hopped up beside me, his presence both grounding and reassuring.

"Do you think these charms are meant for us specifically?" I asked him, seeking his insight.

He tilted his head thoughtfully. "Could be," he mused. "But it feels more like a broad attack—a way to incapacitate any magically sensitive individuals who might get too close."

I frowned at that possibility. It made sense—the charm would serve as an effective deterrent for anyone investigating Jacob's murder who had magical abilities.

"We'll tell Thorn everything once he gets back," I decided aloud. My resolve strengthened with each word spoken. "We'll ask him to search for it—carefully."

Meri nodded solemnly before offering a sliver of levity. "And then maybe he can fetch us a snack."

I managed a weak chuckle at his attempt to lighten the mood before standing. "I'm not going back in there until Thorn finds that charm," I declared firmly.

"Good plan." Meri said. "In the meantime, let's walk around some more—clear our heads."

We walked aimlessly for a while around Clara's neighborhood streets lined with quaint houses and well-kept lawns. As we moved further away from Clara's house and its hidden misery charm, clarity began seeping back into my thoughts like ink slowly staining clear water.

I started piecing together everything we knew so far about Jacob's death and how each person connected might fit into this tangled web of envy and resentment.

"Clara's obsession with Jacob... Martha's secret affair... Essie's stolen hybrid strain... It all intertwines somehow," I murmured aloud as if saying it would help make sense of it all.

Meri trotted alongside me as we turned back toward where Thorn would eventually return—hopefully with Clara in tow—and hopefully unharmed.

"And whoever is using these charms is either trying very hard to point fingers or cover their tracks." My fingers curled into fists at my sides—the frustration at being unable to protect those around me was gnawing at me.

Meri bumped against my leg again—a small gesture but one filled with understanding and support.

The weight of despair lingered on the edges of my consciousness, like a bad dream I couldn't fully wake from. Meri's presence, usually a beacon of sarcastic comfort, was a muted force beside me as we paced the quiet street. The sunshine did little to warm the chill of anxiety that had settled in my bones.

"Kinsley!" The voice shattered the oppressive silence that had enveloped us. Thorn was back. He jumped out, his face a mix of relief and concern as he strode toward us.

"He's in one piece," Meri whispered, as if reading my most pressing fear.

"Clara's in jail," Thorn announced, confirming what I'd hoped to hear. "I caught up with her trying to hide out at a friend's place across town."

I exhaled a breath I didn't realize I'd been holding. "Are you okay?" I asked, scanning him for any sign of injury or distress.

"I'm fine," he assured me, his hand finding mine and giving it a reassuring squeeze. "You two should get in the cruiser. I'll drive you home."

I hesitated, glancing back at Clara's house with trepidation. "There's a misery charm somewhere inside," I explained, the words tumbling out in a rush. "It's why we walked across the street—to get away from it."

Thorn's brow furrowed in understanding. "Wait here," he said with determination. "I'll find it."

As Thorn disappeared back into Clara's house, Meri and I huddled on the curb. His tail wrapped around my ankle—a small gesture that grounded me more than he probably knew.

Minutes stretched into an eternity until Thorn finally emerged from the house, his expression grim but victorious. In his hand was a small velvet box that seemed far too innocuous to hold such malevolence.

"It was in a jewelry box, tucked away in a back drawer," he explained as he approached us.

"Smart hiding place," Meri commented dryly. "For all her orderliness, Clara knew how to bury her secrets deep."

Thorn nodded and made his way to the trunk of his cruiser, placing the velvet box carefully inside before closing it with a decisive thud.

"We can't destroy it yet," he said as he returned to us. "We need to ask Clara if she knows what it is."

A shiver ran down my spine at the thought of confronting Clara with her own dark tools. But Thorn was right, we needed answers.

Chapter 16

I huddled in the passenger seat of Thorn's cruiser, Meri perched beside me, his eyes wide and watchful. The car's motion didn't quite distract from the sense of unease that had settled in my chest, a cold stone where warmth should have been. Thorn had put the charm in the trunk, but its presence still crept through the metal like tendrils of ice water, threatening to seep into my thoughts.

Meri leaned closer, his fur brushing against my arm. "Bad enough we have to ride with that thing."

I nodded, trying to focus on the lights flashing by outside. "It's just a little longer. We'll be at the station soon."

The drive felt endless, each second stretching out as the charm's influence pressed against us like an invisible weight. I could feel it calling to me, urging me to reach out and let it take hold completely. I shivered and drew my cardigan tighter around me.

Finally, we arrived at the station. Thorn parked and went around to retrieve the charm from the trunk. I took a deep breath as he walked away with it, feeling the pressure ease slightly without its proximity.

"We'll stay here for a moment," I told Meri as we watched Thorn enter the building. "Let him get it inside and settled."

Meri's tail twitched in agreement. "No need to rush into that cloud of despair."

We made our way inside after giving it a few minutes. The familiar walls of the station did little to comfort me now; I could feel that charm's presence like a shadow hanging over everything.

In the interrogation room, Thorn began the interview with Clara. She was clearly agitated, her hands fidgeting in her lap as she sat across from him.

Meri and I took our positions at the far end of the observation room, as far from that wretched charm as we could get without leaving entirely. The glass between us didn't block out its influence entirely, but putting physical distance between us helped keep its grip at bay.

Thorn was speaking in low tones, his voice calm and even as he questioned Clara about her actions leading up to Jacob's death. Jeremy sat next to him silently observing.

"Clara," Thorn began with a stern yet controlled demeanor, "we found something rather disturbing among your possessions—a charm similar to one found under suspicious circumstances elsewhere. Can you tell us where you got this?"

Clara glanced down at her hands before meeting Thorn's gaze with a flicker of defiance. "I found it in

Jacob's workshop," she admitted after a pause heavy enough to feel even through the glass. "A couple of days before... before everything happened."

Leaning against the cool wall of the observation room, I watched Thorn's posture, upright and alert, as he continued his interrogation of Clara. Meri settled next to me, his tail flicking with every lie we sensed.

"Why were you in Jacob's workshop?" Thorn's question was direct, his eyes never leaving Clara's face.

Clara hesitated, her fingers intertwining nervously. "I wanted to see if he had sketched out his plan for the competition," she confessed, a hint of shame creeping into her voice. "I thought maybe if I knew what he was planning, I could... I don't know... adjust my own design to stand out more."

"And this charm?" Thorn motioned towards the small object lying on the table between them. "Did you understand what it was when you took it?"

"No," Clara replied quickly, a little too quickly. "I thought it might have been some sort of good luck charm for Jacob. So, I took it—thought maybe it would throw him off his game."

Meri's snort was soft but clear beside me. He didn't believe her, neither did I. Thorn gave a nod to

Jeremy, who promptly picked up the charm and left the room.

As soon as the door closed behind him, a wave of relief washed over me like a warm breeze chasing away the chill of winter. I hadn't realized how much that charm had been affecting me until it was gone. Meri shook his head as if clearing the last vestiges of fog from his thoughts.

"Feel that?" I whispered to him.

"Like shedding a hundred-pound cloak," Meri muttered back.

We assumed Jeremy took the charm to the evidence room. The distance between us and that piece of dark magic seemed enough to shield us from its depressive influence. My mind felt clearer now, sharper—like emerging from a fog into crisp morning air.

In the interrogation room, Thorn pressed on with his questions while Clara struggled to maintain her composure. The desperation in her eyes told me she knew how much trouble she was in. Yet there was something missing in her story—gaps that we still needed to fill.

Thorn's voice broke through my thoughts again. "Clara, your actions suggest premeditation," he said firmly. "Taking that charm might seem innocent enough on its own, but coupled with everything else we've found..."

"I didn't kill him!" Clara cut him off with an outburst, her face flushed with emotion. "I admit I wanted to beat him in the competition—that's all! It was stupid and petty and now... now Jacob is dead."

I glanced at Thorn, catching a brief flicker of doubt cross his face before he masked it with professionalism again.

"Clara," Thorn said, his voice steady and authoritative, "tell me about Jacob's behavior in the days leading up to the competition."

She hesitated, but then her shoulders dropped slightly, as if she were unburdening herself. "He was different—angry, more so than usual. He came over one morning, just raging at Jonas about trampling his vines."

I frowned at this. It didn't seem like something Jonas would do, especially given how much he cared about his own pumpkin patch, however unsuccessful it was.

"Jonas denied it," Clara continued. "He told Jacob he hadn't set foot on his property, but Jacob wouldn't listen."

Thorn leaned forward slightly. "And you believe Jonas?"

"Of course I do," she snapped back.

As Thorn jotted down notes, I considered what Clara had said. Was it possible that the damage Jacob had been so furious about was Essie's doing? She had admitted to stealing samples from his field after all. I shifted my weight from one foot to the other, feeling a restless energy building within me as I waited for Thorn to wrap up the interrogation.

"Clara," Thorn said with a note of finality in his voice, "you need to stay in town while we continue this investigation."

Her lips twisted into a wry smile. "I live here, Sheriff Wilson. It's not like I have anywhere else to go."

There was no trace of fear in her voice or on her face—not even an ounce of remorse for breaking into Jacob's workshop and stealing from him. Clearly, she didn't understand the gravity of the situation or perhaps she just didn't care.

As we left the observation room, Meri slipped out from under my arm and landed gracefully on the floor beside me. "She doesn't get it," he murmured low enough for only my ears.

"No magic in her," I replied quietly as we walked down the corridor toward Thorn's office. "The charm didn't touch her."

Meri flicked his tail in agreement. "Lucky for her."

Thorn joined us shortly after, looking both exhausted and determined—a combination I'd grown all too familiar with over the years.

"Thoughts?" he asked me as we settled into his office.

I took a moment before answering, piecing together everything we knew so far. "Jacob's anger might not have been directed at Jonas after all," I suggested. "It could've been Essie's handiwork he stumbled upon."

Thorn nodded slowly, considering this angle. "It makes sense," he conceded. "She did admit to being there around that time."

***

I leaned back in the chair across from Thorn's desk, tapping a finger against my lips as the pieces started to fall into place. "The charm," I began, glancing over at Meri who was curled up on the windowsill, his eyes sharp and attentive. "It's supposed to incapacitate someone with magic, right?"

Thorn nodded, his brow furrowed. "That's what we've gathered so far."

"But Jacob," I continued, a theory bubbling to the surface of my thoughts, "he was affected by the charm too. It didn't paralyze him with despair like it did us, but it fouled his mood."

Meri's ears perked up and he uncoiled from his perch, pacing the sill. "That would explain why the charm found near him wasn't as potent. If he only had a smidgen of magic, it might not have hit him as hard."

Thorn leaned forward, resting his elbows on his desk. "So you think Martha could be behind the charms?"

I nodded slowly. "It's just a theory at this point, but if Martha was trying to sabotage the other carvers... and she had enough magic to help Jacob's pumpkins grow..." I trailed off, not wanting to voice the darker implication of my thoughts.

Thorn ran a hand through his hair. "That she'd commit murder? To clear the way for Jonas?" He didn't sound convinced but also didn't dismiss it outright.

I sighed and looked out the window, watching as afternoon settled over Coventry like a soft blanket. The idea that Martha could harm Jacob seemed outlandish; she had cared for him deeply. Yet love and guilt could twist people into doing unimaginable things.

Meri jumped down from the sill and sauntered over to us. "Martha's magic is gentle—kitchen witchery and plant spells," he said thoughtfully. "But that doesn't mean she couldn't have learned something darker along the way."

Chapter 17

The sun dipped low, brushing the horizon with a warm, golden hue as Thorn, Meri, and I made our way back to the Thompson farm. The events of the day churned in my mind, leaving a bitter trail of suspicion and uncertainty. We were close, I could feel it—the truth hovered just beyond our reach, teasing us with fleeting shadows and half-heard whispers.

We parked the cruiser at the end of the gravel driveway, the crunch of stones under tires breaking the evening stillness. The Thompson farm spread out before us, a patchwork of thriving greenery and magic-touched soil. But now, there was an undercurrent of tension that even the vibrant blooms couldn't mask.

We stepped out of the car, and I could feel Meri tense in my bag, his body rigid against my side. He was as ready as I was to unearth whatever secrets were buried here.

"Remember," Thorn said, his blue eyes meeting mine with a steely resolve. "We're not accusing anyone. We just want answers."

I nodded, clenching my jaw to steel myself against the rising tide of emotion. This wasn't just about finding a murderer, it was about untangling a web of family secrets that had bound these people in knots for years.

We hadn't taken more than a few steps toward the house when Jonas emerged from around the corner of the barn. His figure cut a sharp silhouette against the setting sun—tall and imposing, with an intensity that seemed to ripple through the air around him.

"Get off our property," Jonas's voice boomed across the yard, his hands balled into fists at his sides. He stalked toward us with purposeful strides, his eyes locked on Thorn.

Thorn held up his hands in a gesture of peace. "Jonas, we need to talk. It's important."

"I said leave!" Jonas's shout carried a raw edge of protectiveness that gave me pause. He stopped short in front of us, his chest heaving with barely restrained anger.

I stepped forward then, knowing my presence often had a calming effect on tense situations—a remnant of my coven leader days. "Jonas," I began softly, "we're not here to cause trouble. We just want to understand what happened to Jacob."

His gaze flicked to me then back to Thorn. The muscles in his jaw worked as he ground his teeth together. "You've got no right poking around here," he spat out.

"Jonas," Thorn interjected firmly but without aggression, "we found something—a charm meant to cause harm to those with magic." He paused for effect and continued, "It's linked to Jacob's murder."

The mention of magic seemed to strike a chord in Jonas; he faltered for a moment before regaining his composure.

"I don't know anything about any charms," he growled.

Meri poked his head out from my bag then and fixed Jonas with his piercing gold eyes. "Lies don't suit you," he said sharply.

Jonas recoiled slightly at Meri's words as if they'd physically struck him. It was clear he hadn't expected Meri—a cat—to speak so candidly or at all.

"We think Martha might be involved," I said gently but firmly. "She may have been trying to give you an advantage in the competition."

"I don't need her help!" Jonas's voice cracked with emotion. He turned away from us briefly before spinning back around, his face contorted in anguish. "She always meddles—always trying to fix things!"

The confrontation with Jonas was like walking a tightrope over a chasm of raw, unchecked emotion. His anger, an almost tangible force, rippled through the air. But it wasn't just anger; it was a deep-seated hurt that he wore like armor, a protective barrier against the world.

I held my ground, feeling Thorn's steady presence beside me and Meri's weight against my side. My heart ached for Jonas, caught in the crossfire of secrets and lies that had defined his life without his consent.

The sound of hurried footsteps broke the tense silence, and we all turned to see Martha hurrying toward us, her face etched with concern. She must have heard the raised voices from her garden.

"Jonas, what's going on?" Martha called out as she approached, her eyes darting between us with a mix of fear and confusion.

I took a deep breath before speaking. "Martha, we need to talk about the charms—the ones meant to harm those with magic."

At the mention of the charms, Martha's face crumpled like a paper lantern in the rain. Tears welled up in her eyes, spilling over her cheeks as she clasped her hands together.

"I... I can't keep this inside any longer," she sobbed, the words tumbling out in a torrent of regret and sorrow. "I did it. I made those charms."

Jonas's eyes widened in shock as he turned to his mother. "You... what? Why would you do that?"

Martha reached out for him, but he stepped back, recoiling from her touch as if it burned.

"I wanted to give you a chance at winning," she cried. "You've been so unhappy, so angry all the time. Your magic—it's been twisted by your emotions. I thought if you could just win once..."

She trailed off, gasping for breath between sobs. It was a confession born from desperation—a mother's misguided attempt to heal her son's wounded spirit.

"You have magic?" Jonas's voice was barely above a whisper, but it carried all the weight of his newfound realization.

Martha nodded slowly. "Yes, my boy. You do, too. And it's powerful—more powerful than you know."

Jonas staggered back as if struck by an invisible force. The truth hit him hard and fast—a truth that reshaped his entire understanding of himself and his place in the world.

"I didn't know how else to help," Martha continued, wiping at her tears with trembling hands. "When Jacob refused to drop out of the competition... I made stronger charms."

I stepped closer to Martha, placing a hand on her shoulder in an attempt to offer some comfort amidst the turmoil.

"You planted them in the sheds?" I asked softly.

Martha nodded again. "Yes," she whispered hoarsely. "In every shed but Jonas's and Clara's."

The admission hung between us like a dark cloud threatening to burst.

"And you were hoping this would... what? Improve Jonas's chances of winning?" Thorn interjected gently but firmly.

Martha looked at him through tear-streaked eyes. "Yes," she admitted with a nod. "I thought if he could just win—if he could feel that joy and pride—it might start to heal whatever darkness has taken root in him."

It was clear now; Martha's love for her son had driven her to take drastic—and dangerous—measures.

"And when Jacob refused..." I prompted softly, not wanting to push her too hard but needing to understand the full extent of what happened.

"When he refused," Martha said through gritted teeth, "I decided I had to do whatever it took." Her voice broke on the last word as another wave of tears overtook her.

Jonas stood motionless during his mother's confession, his face unreadable. The revelation that magic ran through his veins seemed to leave him reeling—a man unmoored from everything he believed about himself.

Martha reached out again toward Jonas; this time he didn't move away but didn't accept her hand either—suspended in indecision and shock.

"Ma," Jonas said finally, his voice hoarse with emotion. "Why didn't you tell me? All this time... all these years..."

"I was afraid," Martha admitted, looking at him with eyes full of regret. "Afraid you'd resent me more for keeping it from you than for not having magic at all."

I could see Thorn shifting uncomfortably beside me; this family drama was far beyond our usual scope of law enforcement work.

I felt a knot twist in my stomach as Thorn turned to Martha, his expression a blend of duty and regret. "Martha, I'm going to have to arrest you for murder," he said, the words hanging heavy in the air. "When your charms didn't make Jacob withdraw from the competition, it seems you took things a step further."

Martha's face crumpled, her hands shaking as she clutched them to her chest. "No, Thorn," she pleaded, her voice raw with emotion. "I wouldn't—I couldn't do that. I made those charms out of desperation, but murder? I loved Jacob."

Jonas stood beside his mother, a statue of confliction. His eyes darted between Thorn and Martha. For a moment, silence stretched taut around us, before he took a shuddering breath and stepped forward.

"I can't let you do this," Jonas said, his voice laced with anguish. "I saw Clara coming out of Jacob's shed that night." He paused, swallowing hard. "When I looked inside... I saw Jacob's body. I knew Clara had killed him."

A chill raced down my spine at his admission. My heart ached for Jonas—torn between love and justice, trying to protect the woman he cared for while standing on the precipice of letting his own mother take the fall for a crime she didn't commit.

"Why didn't you come forward sooner?" Thorn asked, his tone gentle yet probing.

Jonas's jaw tightened as he fought against the emotions threatening to spill over. "I thought I could handle it—protect Clara and keep this family from falling apart." He looked at Martha with eyes full of sorrow. "But I can't let you take the blame for something you didn't do."

Martha reached out to Jonas then, her touch no longer rejected as he leaned into her embrace—a mother and son bound by love and shared pain.

I stepped back, giving them space to process the revelation while keeping an eye on Thorn as he processed what Jonas had just revealed. It was clear we needed to revisit Clara's involvement with fresh eyes—her obsession with Jacob's work had already raised red flags.

"Jonas," Thorn began after giving them a moment together, "we need to go over everything you saw that night—every detail matters now."

Jonas nodded solemnly, wiping away the remnants of tears with the back of his hand. He squared his shoulders as if preparing for battle and looked Thorn directly in the eyes.

"I'll tell you everything," he promised.

Chapter 18

The drive back to the station was silent, thick with unspoken words and the weight of what we'd just learned. Jonas, in the backseat with Thorn driving, stared out the window, his face etched with a mixture of guilt and relief. Martha sat beside Jonas, her hands clasped tightly in her lap, her knuckles white as bone. I could almost feel the tumultuous storm brewing within Jonas as he sat next to his mother.

Once we arrived at the station, Thorn led Martha and Jonas to separate rooms to get their official statements. I waited outside, my mind racing. The pieces were falling into place, each one casting a darker shadow over Clara Greenway.

When Thorn emerged from the interrogation room after speaking with Martha, his face was grave. "She's sticking to her story," he said. "Claims she only wanted to help Jonas win by making those charms. She's adamant she didn't kill Jacob."

"And Jonas?" I asked.

"He's a wreck," Thorn replied. "But he confirmed seeing Clara leaving Jacob's shed that night."

I nodded, my heart sinking. Clara's web of obsession had ensnared not only her but those she claimed to love.

***

Thorn had Jeremy bring Clara into the station. She was placed in an interrogation room, and I joined Thorn in questioning her.

"Clara Greenway," he began as we stepped into the room where she sat cuffed, "we have statements from both Martha and Jonas Thompson placing you at Jacob Appleton's shed the night he was killed."

Her eyes flickered with something dark and unreadable before she masked it with indignation. "Jonas would never—"

"Essie also saw you," I cut in gently, watching as her façade cracked just a hair.

Clara looked between us, defiance burning in her gaze. But beneath that fire, I saw it—the flicker of fear.

Thorn leaned forward, his voice steady but commanding. "Clara, if there's something you need to tell us, now is the time."

She hesitated, and for a moment I thought she might break then and there. But then she straightened her back and shook her head.

"I don't know what you're talking about," she said flatly.

I exchanged a glance with Thorn. We'd seen this dance before—the back and forth of guilt and innocence playing out like some macabre ballet.

"Jonas said he found Jacob dead after you left his shed," Thorn pressed on. "And Essie's testimony about seeing you there is corroborated by several others who noticed you acting strangely around that time."

Clara's eyes darted away for a fraction of a second before meeting mine again. "They're lying," she spat out. But there was desperation in her voice now—a plea for us to disbelieve what was increasingly obvious.

"We also found the charm in your possession," I said softly, hoping to coax the truth from her like coaxing a butterfly from its cocoon. "The same type that nearly crushed Roger under despair and which you claimed was from Jacob's workshop."

"I—I thought it was his good luck charm," Clara stammered, but her conviction was fading fast.

Thorn stood up straighter, his presence filling the room like an unyielding force. "We've seen your garage too," he added. "The carvings... they tell their own story."

Her jaw tightened; I could see the muscles work beneath her skin as she grappled with reality closing in around her.

"I wanted to be the best," Clara finally whispered after what felt like an eternity. Her voice broke on each word as if they were shards of glass cutting their way out of her throat.

"And Jacob?" Thorn prodded gently but firmly.

Tears brimmed in Clara's eyes—a dam ready to burst—but she held them back with sheer willpower.

"I just wanted to see what he was planning for the competition," she said hoarsely. "I never meant for any of this to happen."

"But it did happen," Thorn said quietly.

I watched Clara from across the table, her hands cuffed in front of her, her eyes darting around the room as if seeking an escape from the truth that was closing in. Thorn sat beside me, his posture a blend of professionalism and empathy. The silence was heavy, oppressive, and it was only a matter of time before it shattered.

"I didn't go there to hurt him," Clara finally said, her voice quivering like the last leaf on a tree bracing for winter. "I just... I needed to learn from him."

"Learn from Jacob?" I prompted, my tone softer than Thorn's. I knew that sometimes a gentler approach could pry open the tightest lids.

She nodded vigorously, as if trying to convince herself as much as us. "Yes, I thought if he could just show me... show me how he did it, I could finally be better. Better than him. Better for Jonas."

"And what did Jacob say when you asked him?" Thorn's question was direct but not unkind.

Clara's face twisted into a mask of pain and anger as she recalled the moment. "He laughed at me," she spat out, her voice rising in pitch. "He told me he'd never help me—never help anyone who had anything to do with Jonas."

I leaned forward slightly, maintaining eye contact with Clara. "And how did that make you feel?"

She sucked in a breath and held it before releasing it in a rush. "Angry... so angry. And envious." Her eyes were wells of emotion now—remorse, fury, sorrow all swirling together.

Thorn's hand brushed against mine in silent support as we listened to Clara unravel.

"He said I had no talent," she continued, the words tumbling out faster now. "That he wouldn't waste his time on Jonas's untalented girlfriend. I should have known every time he said something nice or encouraging to me, it was an act."

The room seemed to grow colder with each word she uttered—a chill that seeped into my bones.

"And then?" Thorn pressed.

"I just snapped." Clara's hands shook visibly now, and I noticed her biting her lip so hard it was on the verge of bleeding. "I picked up one of his carving tools and... and hit him from behind."

I felt Thorn stiffen beside me; this was the confession we'd been waiting for.

"He fell without making a sound," Clara murmured, staring down at her hands as if seeing them for the first time. "And then... then I carved him." Her voice was barely audible now, a ghostly whisper that hung in the air between us.

"You carved Jacob's body to prove your skill?" It wasn't so much a question as it was a plea for confirmation of the horror we were hearing.

"Yes," she whispered. "To show that I was better... that I could be better than him."

"And after?" My voice sounded distant even to my own ears.

"I left." A tear escaped down her cheek, tracing a path through her foundation. "I didn't know Jonas had seen me. He must hate me now." She lifted her gaze to meet mine—a plea for understanding or forgiveness, I couldn't tell which.

"Anything else?" Thorn asked gently.

Clara nodded slowly, another tear following the first. "I wish Jonas knew how much I love him... that everything I did was for us."

Thorn took over then, asking Clara to recount every detail of that night—and then to write it out. He wanted to leave no room for her to wiggle out of her confession.

As Clara spoke, my mind raced with questions about love and obsession—how one could twist into the other so seamlessly until actions born from affection became monstrous deeds cloaked in darkness.

I felt Thorn's gaze on me—a silent acknowledgment that this case had burrowed under our skin and settled into our thoughts long after we'd leave this room.

"Kinsley," he said quietly once Clara had finished speaking and sat there looking smaller than ever before—defeated by her own handiwork.

"Yes?" My voice sounded steady despite the turmoil inside.

"Let's step outside for a moment."

We excused ourselves from the interrogation room and found solace in the quiet corridor outside. Thorn looked at me with concern etched across his features—a rare crack in his composed facade.

"Are you all right?" he asked.

The question took me by surprise—not because he asked it but because I wasn't sure how to answer truthfully without revealing the depth of my distress over this case—the cruelty, the wasted talent, and lives irreparably broken by jealousy and misplaced love.

"I will be," I replied after a pause that lingered too long between us. "It's just... this one got to me."

"Let's get back in there and finish this."

Chapter 19

I stood there, arms crossed, watching Clara wilt under Thorn's relentless questioning. Her confession echoed in the sterile room, and the atmosphere was heavy with a cocktail of relief and despair. She looked smaller somehow, her shoulders hunched, her eyes dimmed from the fierce spark they held when she spoke of pumpkin carving.

Thorn's gaze never wavered from Clara as he processed her admission. The man had a way of being present that often intimidated even the hardest criminals. But it wasn't his presence that startled me next—it was the abrupt slam of the door.

Jonas Thompson barreled into the interrogation room, bypassing protocol and probably a couple of officers along the way. His face was a mask of anguish, and as far as I could figure, he must have snuck into the observation room. He probably watched the entire interrogation.

"Clara!" he exclaimed, rushing to her side.

She recoiled at first, as if his voice yanked her from one nightmare into another. But then something shifted in her eyes—a flicker of recognition, perhaps a glimmer of hope.

"I love you too," Jonas declared breathlessly, gripping the metal table for support. "I'm sorry all we've done is argue recently."

Thorn and I exchanged a look, his eyebrow arching in silent question. Should we intervene? But there was something undeniably raw about this moment—a sense of finality that made us both hesitate.

Clara's eyes welled with tears, and she looked up at Jonas with an expression that tugged at my heart despite everything. It was as if in this instant, all the madness fell away to reveal two people desperately clinging to each other amidst the wreckage they'd created.

"I never wanted any of this," Clara murmured, her voice barely above a whisper. "I just wanted to be great."

"You are great," Jonas said fiercely. "You're the most talented carver I've ever known. I've been so caught up in my own issues with Jacob that I couldn't see how much pressure I put on you."

The confession hung between them like a fragile truce, one that could shatter with any sudden movement or harsh word.

"Jonas," Clara began, her voice steadying with resolve. "I didn't do it for me—I did it for us."

I could almost hear Thorn's jaw clench from where I stood behind the glass. The gravity of what she was saying wasn't lost on any of us—she killed for love, or at least that's what she believed.

Jonas reached out and took Clara's hands in his own. They were both shaking, their fingers interlocking like pieces searching for their rightful place.

"I know," he said softly. "And I can't tell you how much that means to me." His thumbs brushed over her knuckles in a tender gesture that felt so out of place in this cold room.

They seemed lost in their own world for those moments—a bubble where their twisted romance could exist unchallenged by reality or consequence.

But reality has a way of asserting itself—especially when you're standing in an interrogation room after confessing to murder—and Thorn stepped forward to remind them of just that.

"Jonas Thompson," he said firmly but not unkindly. "You need to step back."

The couple jolted as if waking from a dream. Thorn's voice grounded us all back into the grimness of our surroundings.

"I have to take Clara into custody," Thorn continued, his tone apologetic but resolute.

Jonas released Clara's hands slowly, as if letting go was an act requiring tremendous strength. He nodded once at Thorn—acknowledgment and surrender wrapped into one heavy gesture—and stepped away from Clara.

Jeremy's grip was firm on Jonas's arm, but not unkind, as he guided him out of the interrogation room. Jonas stumbled slightly as he exited, his eyes red-rimmed and vacant. He looked like a man who had just come to terms with the weight of his reality crashing down around him. And then Martha appeared.

She moved toward Jonas with open arms, her own eyes glistening with unshed tears. "Oh, Jonas," she murmured as she embraced him.

"I couldn't let her take the fall alone," Jonas confessed, his voice thick with emotion. "She needs to know how much she means to me. What she did... it was wrong, but my brother... I doubt we ever would've gotten along."

Martha held him at arm's length now, looking into his eyes with pain and understanding. "But you need to know your worth too, Jonas," she said softly. "I might have helped Jacob's pumpkins grow, but I helped you too. I was always there for you."

I stood by silently, my heart going out to them both. Martha's revelation about helping Jacob's pumpkins grow was hardly a surprise given everything else that had come to light.

"Yes, I helped Jacob," Martha repeated like her words were a spell. "But I tried for you too, Jonas." Her voice broke on his name. "Your anger and bitterness seeped into everything you touched—it overpowered my magic."

Jonas closed his eyes for a moment, a single tear escaping down his cheek. "I never meant to let it control me."

Martha reached up to wipe the tear away gently. "You have your own magic inside you, son," she said firmly. "But it's tainted by your resentments. Let them go."

Jonas nodded slowly, a quiet promise in his posture. "I'll try," he said simply. "For Clara... for myself."

I watched Thorn as he joined us, his face somber. In his hand was a piece of paper—Clara's official confession. He walked over to where Jonas and Martha stood, their arms still wrapped around each other in a maternal embrace.

"I have Clara's full confession," Thorn said gently. "I'm turning her over to the state police along with this document."

Jonas let out a strangled sob at the words. He buried his face in his mother's shoulder as his body shook. Martha held him tightly, tears glistening in her own eyes.

Thorn hesitated, as if debating whether to continue. But we all knew what had to come next. "Jonas," he began, "I'm afraid I'll also have to bring you in."

At this, Jonas lifted his head, surprise mingling with the anguish on his face.

"You withheld valuable information by not coming forward right away after seeing Clara leave that shed," Thorn explained. His tone was kind but firm. "There will be consequences for that."

"But I—I was just trying to protect her," Jonas stammered.

Thorn nodded. "I understand. But the law doesn't see it that way."

Jonas looked back and forth between Thorn and his mother, uncertainty etched across his features. Martha cupped his face in her hands.

"It's okay, sweetheart," she soothed. "We'll get through this."

Jonas nodded, a bit of resolve entering his eyes. He straightened and turned to Thorn.

"All right then," he said quietly. "I'm ready."

Thorn motioned for Jeremy to come over. As he escorted Jonas out, Martha called after him.

"I love you, Jonas. Stay strong."

Jonas managed a small smile back at her. "I love you too, Mom."

Then he was gone, the door closing heavily behind him. Martha stood there a moment, looking lost. Then she sank into a chair, putting her face in her hands. I walked over and sat down next to her.

"He's a good man, Martha," I said gently. "He'll get through this."

She lifted her head, eyes rimmed red but determined.

"You're right," she replied. "My boy has always been strong, even if he did lose his way for a bit." She patted my hand. "Thank you, dear."

I smiled at her reassuringly. We sat in silence for a few moments before Thorn came back over. He crouched down in front of Martha, his expression solemn.

"I know this is difficult," he began. "But I promise we'll do everything we can for Jonas and Clara both. The law must run its course, but there's hope too."

Martha regarded him thoughtfully. "You've always been reasonable, Sheriff," she said finally. "I appreciate that. And I know my Jonas - he'll face what's coming with courage."

Thorn nodded. "I believe that too. Now why don't I have someone drive you home?"

Martha agreed, and Thorn called over a deputy. As we watched her leave, I slipped my hand into Thorn's.

"That was nicely handled," I told him.

He sighed. "This whole case has been a mess from the start. I just want to see some justice, but not at the expense of compassion."

I squeezed his hand. "That's why you're so good at your job. You understand that balance."

Thorn gave me a small, grateful smile. But it faded as his gaze moved to the interrogation room where Clara waited.

"I should go update her on everything," he said heavily.

"Do you want me there too?" I asked.

He considered it a moment then shook his head. "No, I'll handle this solo. Why don't you head home and I'll meet you there soon?"

I agreed, knowing he needed to do this last difficult task on his own. I gave him a quick kiss, wishing I could erase the weariness from his eyes. But I knew the only cure for that was time.

"See you at home," I said. "I love you."

"Love you too."

With that, we parted ways. I headed out into the parking lot, breathing in the fresh night air. The pumpkin festival still twinkled in the distance, a strange contrast to the turmoil that had just played out.

As I drove home, I felt bone-tired yet wired all at once. My mind spun through everything that had happened - the shocking murder, the dark magic, the family revelations. We had our culprit, yet my life still had loose ends.

Chapter 20

I leaned against the cool metal of Thorn's cruiser, watching as the final echoes of chaos from the past few days began to settle into a subdued murmur. The professional pumpkin carving competition was canceled, the HappyTummy chain having no choice but to pull the plug due to the diminished number of entrants. Yet, Coventry's spirit proved resilient; townsfolk and visitors alike swarmed to witness the amateur event.

The air was crisp with autumn's chill, scented with cinnamon and nutmeg from nearby stalls peddling all things pumpkin-spiced. A gentle breeze tousled my curly red hair as I watched Hekate and Laney join the other children in front of the judges' table. Despite their young ages, they stood with a maturity that belied their years, eager anticipation written on their faces.

Hekate clutched her little black cloak tighter around her shoulders, her dark eyes gleaming with excitement. Her pumpkin, a sinister concoction of necromantic symbols and haunting figures, had drawn both admiration and a touch of wariness from onlookers. Laney's creation, on the other hand, showcased her studious nature—a meticulously detailed carving of Coventry's crest that echoed her inherent leadership qualities.

The announcement came—a tie for second place between sisters. The crowd erupted into applause as Hekate and Laney were each presented with a ribbon, identical smiles blooming on their faces. It was one of those rare moments when their competitiveness gave way to sisterly pride, each genuinely pleased for the other.

My own entry—a whimsical scene of witches dancing under a harvest moon—remained ribbonless among its peers. A twinge of disappointment nipped at me, quickly dispelled by Thorn's warm hand finding mine.

"Don't worry about it," he whispered with a soft chuckle. "Yours had the most character."

I smiled up at him, grateful for his unwavering support. "I think character is code for 'not good enough for a ribbon,' isn't it?"

Thorn shook his head with an exaggerated sigh. "Not everything is about winning."

His playful nudge led us away from the judging area and toward one of the stalls that boasted an array of treats guaranteed to stick to your ribs—and your fingers.

"Wait here," he said, walking off toward a food stall. He returned with a caramel apple in hand, its thick coating glistening under the festival lights. "For you," he said, presenting it like a prized trophy. "The sweetest consolation prize."

I took a bite, letting the rich caramel offset any lingering hint of disappointment. The apple was crisp and tart, perfectly balanced by its sugary shell—much like how Thorn balanced me in life's ups and downs.

We strolled through the festival together as darkness draped over us like a comforting blanket. The air filled with laughter and music while I savored my treat and Thorn sipped coffee from his travel mug— definitely not from the station's stash he so despised.

"Hey," I said between bites, "you think we should have let Hekate enter a gourd from her poisoner's garden instead? Maybe she would have snagged first place."

Thorn glanced at me sideways, an amused glint in his blue eyes. "Let's not encourage our first-grader to display her deadly flora at public events."

"Fair point," I conceded with a laugh.

As we meandered among pumpkin-laden booths and children darting like frenzied sprites through clusters of adults, I couldn't help but feel an immense sense of pride—not just for Hekate and Laney but for Thorn too. He'd been such an anchor through everything— the investigation into Jacob's murder, my confrontations with Lisa, even our momentary lapses in communication—all while carrying out his duties as sheriff with unwavering dedication.

We paused to watch Hekate and Laney again; they were animatedly discussing their pumpkins with some other children who looked at them both in awe. It warmed my heart to see them so content.

"You know," I mused aloud to Thorn as we watched our daughters from afar, "I think they really could lead the coven someday."

He nodded solemnly but there was a twinkle in his eye that told me he shared my thoughts.

Our peaceful reverie was interrupted by Meri bounding over to us after having slipped away unnoticed earlier in pursuit of some undoubtedly mischievous endeavor involving leftover pumpkin scraps.

"You two look like you're plotting," Meri commented slyly as he sidled up next to us.

"Merely admiring our daughters' diplomacy," I replied with a smile.

Thorn threw an arm around my shoulder as we resumed walking through the festival grounds together.

We were just rounding a corner lined with booths when we spotted Roger and Essie by his trailer, the side of which was painted with an elaborate mural of a pumpkin so lifelike it seemed you could pluck it right off the metal.

Roger was securing something in the back of a pickup truck while Essie organized tools on a fold-out table. They both looked up as we approached.

"Roger, Essie," I called out with a small wave. "Heading out?"

Roger flashed a smile, one that didn't quite reach his eyes but was genuine enough. "Yeah, got the all-clear from the hospital. They said I'm fine now."

Essie nodded in confirmation, her hand lingering on his arm longer than necessary. "I'll keep an eye on him," she said. "We're headed back to work on our own harvest."

There was something different about her— she stood close to Roger, almost protective in her stance, and her eyes held a new light that I hadn't seen before.

Thorn nodded at them. "Glad to hear you're doing better, Roger." His sheriff's scrutiny flickered over them, but his tone was warm.

I studied Essie, trying to read the layers beneath her apparent contentment. Was it possible she felt relief at Jacob's death? It was a dark thought but not unfounded given their history.

As if sensing my line of thought, Essie suddenly met my gaze. "Kinsley," she began hesitantly, "I wanted to tell you... about Jacob's pumpkins."

I raised an eyebrow, prompting her to continue.

"I had those samples analyzed," she said with an unexpected softness in her voice. "The ones I took from Jacob's field."

"And?" Thorn interjected before I could speak.

"They're not my strain." The relief in Essie's voice was tangible as she released a breath she seemed to have been holding for too long.

"Then you can finally move on," I said gently, recognizing this as her moment of closure.

"Yes," Essie smiled, turning towards Roger who looked back at her with an expression that spoke volumes of their growing bond. "And I'll have all the time I need at Roger's farm to perfect it."

Roger put his hand over hers on his arm. "That's right. You focus on your pumpkins, Essie. Let me worry about everything else."

Their exchange wasn't just about pumpkins; it was a promise of support and partnership that had blossomed under adversity—a spark ignited into something more in the wake of tragedy.

Thorn and I shared a glance, acknowledging silently that sometimes life did manage to sprout new beginnings from the ruins of old battles.

"Well," Thorn said after a moment, clapping his hands together once in finality, "we should let you two get on your way then."

"Yes," I echoed. "Take care—and good luck with your strain, Essie."

She nodded gratefully while Roger tipped his hat in farewell before returning to his task.

***

As Thorn steered the cruiser along the winding roads that led back to our house, I found myself gazing out the window at the rolling fields of Coventry. The setting sun cast a golden hue over the landscape, painting it with warm tones that hinted at the promise of tomorrow. We drove in comfortable silence, each lost in our own thoughts about the events that had unfolded over the past few days.

Passing by the Thompson farm, I couldn't help but notice a change in the scenery. The pumpkin patch, which had previously been a sad collection of stunted and twisted gourds, now seemed to be rejuvenated.

The pumpkins were fuller, their vibrant orange skins standing out against the green leaves like flames in a field.

"Look at that," I murmured, nodding toward the patch. "The pumpkins are already looking better."

Thorn slowed down slightly, his eyes following my gaze. "You're right. It's amazing what a little positive energy can do."

I leaned back in my seat, contemplating Jonas's newfound awareness of his magic. "If he can harness his magic into positive feelings, he might grow pumpkins to rival his brother's in the near future."

Thorn nodded solemnly. "It's a shame Jonas and Jacob never reconciled. They could have been a great team."

I sighed, feeling a pang of sadness for what could have been—a relationship mended, a brotherly bond strengthened through shared talent and passion for their craft. But fate had taken a different turn.

"Yeah," I said softly. "It's one of those tragic things—missed opportunities and words left unsaid."

Thorn reached over and gave my hand a reassuring squeeze. We both understood too well how precious and fragile relationships could be.

After a moment of reflection, Thorn cleared his throat. "The state police took Clara into custody earlier this afternoon," he informed me with a note of finality.

I turned to face him, feeling a sense of relief mixed with melancholy. "Good," I said. "She needs to face justice for what she did to Jacob."

"Before long, she'll be in prison where she belongs," Thorn added with a touch of grim satisfaction.

We continued on our way home as twilight settled over Coventry like a gentle cloak. As much as Clara deserved to be held accountable for her actions, I couldn't shake off a sense of sorrow for her too—a young woman so consumed by jealousy and obsession that it led her down such a dark path.

The sky darkened further as we pulled into our driveway. The day's events had taken their toll on us both emotionally and physically, but there was comfort in returning to our sanctuary—our home filled with love and magic.

Chapter 21

I glanced up at our porch, a welcoming beacon to any weary traveler or, in our case, a slightly disheveled family returning from the fair. But tonight, the light was out, leaving the front of our home cloaked in darkness.

I nudged Thorn as he cut the engine. "Looks like someone forgot to change the porch light."

He chuckled, reaching for Laney's booster seat. "You know, with a flick of your wrist and a little incantation, you could've had it shining brighter than a full moon."

"Ah," I teased back as I unbuckled Hekate's seatbelt, "but then you'd miss out on the joys of household maintenance. Where's the fun in that?"

Our playful squabble continued as we ushered the girls inside. The night had been long, and our spirits needed the refuge of our cozy living room. Yet as I crossed the threshold, an icy grip of despair seized me. It was sudden, as if stepping into a hidden snare that tugged at my soul.

Meri's yowl echoed in my mind, not his usual sarcastic snark but a wail that carried an ocean of sorrow. I felt his presence pressing against my consciousness, each thought laced with hopelessness.

Laney's laughter faded into sobs that pierced the heavy air while Hekate's complaints morphed into whines that pulled at my heartstrings. I turned to Thorn for support, only to find him cradling Laney in his arms, confusion etched across his rugged features.

"What's wrong, sweetheart?" he asked gently.

I tried to speak up, to warn him of the shadow that loomed behind him—tall and ominous—but my voice was a prisoner to the despair. The words died in my throat as lethargy wrapped its cold fingers around me. What was the point? Did any of it even matter?

The darkness seeped into the corners of my mind, thick and cloying, like ink dripping into water. I could sense Thorn's unease as he tried to soothe Laney, but his words felt distant, muffled by the overwhelming gloom that had settled over us. I needed to shake this feeling, to warn him, but my body felt like it was encased in lead.

And then she appeared—Lisa, her presence slicing through the haze like a knife. She stood in the doorway, a silhouette against the dim light from outside. Her hand moved swiftly, purposefully, and before I could even process her intention, a sharp crackling sound pierced the air.

Thorn's body jerked violently as the taser's prongs found their mark. Laney cried out—a short, startled sound—and then silence. My heart raced, fear for them overtaking the numbing despair. I reached out to grab Laney as Thorn's arms went limp, but Lisa was relentless. She held down the trigger until he crumpled to the floor, a fallen titan in our own home.

"Thorn!" My voice finally broke free from its prison of dread as I knelt beside him. His eyes were closed, his face contorted in pain. Laney lay beside him, her small frame shaking but thankfully conscious.

"I'm so sorry," Lisa whispered to Thorn's prone figure, her voice laced with a delusion of affection. "I'll make it up to you later."

Make it up to him? The absurdity of her words stoked a fire within me—a fierce protectiveness that burned away the last vestiges of darkness. I cradled Laney in my arms, feeling her warmth against me as Meri hissed furiously from behind us.

As Lisa stepped over Thorn's body, the room seemed to tilt, reality warping at the edges. I held Laney tight, her small form trembling in my arms as the light from outside threw Lisa's shadow long and sinister across the floor. My gaze darted to Hekate, my little necromancer, her maturity beyond her years now crumbled into a child's fear as she huddled in the corner.

"You're not going to win this," I spat, my voice laced with venom I rarely let surface.

Lisa's lips twisted into a smug smile. "Oh, Kinsley," she cooed, her tone sickeningly sweet, "I've been listening, learning. Since you flaunted your magic, I've been digging. Digging for a way to use it against you."

My mind raced. This wasn't just a woman scorned; this was someone who'd been playing a long game. "You knew about magic," I reminded her through gritted teeth. "You begged for a love spell once."

She waved away the memory like it was nothing more than an annoying fly. "Desperate hope," she said with a dismissive flick of her wrist. "I never really expected that to work."

Bonkers waddled over to Laney as I set her down and put myself between her and Lisa. His orange bulk somehow comforting as he climbed onto her lap. His purring vibrated through the room—a small but defiant sound against the tide of despair.

Lisa pulled something from her pocket, holding it up for me to see—a misery charm, glinting maliciously in the low light. "I heard about the charms through gossip... and a friend at the police station." She stepped closer, and I could feel its pull—the amplified misery that clung to it like cobwebs.

Meri's eyes met mine across the room. The ancient witch within that black cat form was fighting his own battle against the charm's influence, but there was an understanding there—a silent command passing between us.

I didn't need to speak; Meri knew what he had to do—protect Hekate. With surprising agility for his size, he leaped toward my youngest daughter.

Lisa edged closer still, malice etched in every line of her face. "Someone with loose ethics helped me amp up the magic," she said proudly. "Admire how well it works now."

The room seemed to darken around us, each shadow deepening as despair threatened to choke me once more. But anger was a powerful antidote to hopelessness—anger and love.

Hekate's soft sobs cut through everything else—the most heart-wrenching sound I'd ever heard from my child—and it ignited something primal within me.

"No!" My voice broke free from any restraint I had left as Meri reached Hekate's side. He rubbed against her leg in an attempt to ground her—to remind her she wasn't alone.

Lisa took another step forward, the charm outstretched in her hand like an offering of death itself.

The pull was strong; I could feel its tendrils wrapping around my thoughts, trying to drag me under again.

But I looked at Laney—her wide eyes finding strength in Bonkers' steady purr—I looked at Meri as he stood guard by Hekate—and I knew surrender wasn't an option.

Despair had settled over me like a thick fog, seeping into my bones and weighing down each breath I took. Lisa stood before me, Thorn's service pistol in her hand, a sinister smile on her lips. The darkness from the misery charm in her other hand was almost tangible, wrapping around me, urging me to give up, to succumb to the nothingness that promised to engulf me.

"How do you think this will win you Thorn's heart?" I managed to choke out.

Lisa's smile widened as she cocked her head to the side. "I already have his heart," she said with unnerving confidence. "He just needs help recognizing it." She took a step closer, the gun unwavering in her grip. "And as for the girls," she continued, glancing briefly at Laney and Hekate, "they'll come around. I can be very... persuasive."

The thought of this woman trying to take my place— my family—ignited a spark of defiance within me. My girls needed their mother; Thorn needed his wife, not some deluded interloper with a penchant for manipulation and magic theft.

As if on cue, Meri brushed against my ankle, his presence grounding me further. His touch was a reminder of the strength that lay within me—a strength no charm could fully extinguish.

With each passing second, the despair began to lift like mist under the morning sun. I could feel the power within me stirring once again, ready to burst forth and protect my family from this threat.

Just as I prepared to unleash a blast of magic at Lisa, her body started to convulse. Her confident stance faltered as spasms racked her frame. The pistol clattered to the floor as she crumpled into an uncontrolled heap of twitching limbs.

Thorn was suddenly there beside her, his taser in hand and his face set in grim determination. He moved quickly but carefully as he secured his weapon and snapped handcuffs around her wrists.

Without a word, he scooped up the misery charm and strode outside with it. The absence of its oppressive aura was immediate, relief washed over me like a wave crashing onto shore.

I gathered Laney into my arms as Meri settled protectively by Hekate's side. The chaos had erupted so quickly—too quickly for any child to process—and now they clung to each other, their world shaken but still intact.

***

I watched as Jeremy and a couple more deputies
pulled up to our house, their lights painting the night
with streaks of red and blue. Thorn stood on the
porch, his hand on his holster, a silent sentinel
guarding our little family as chaos had unfolded
inside. As the officers filed out of their vehicles,
Jeremy at the lead, I couldn't help but feel a wave of
gratitude for the life we'd built—chaotic as it could
be.

"Kinsley?" Jeremy's voice was gentle but firm as he
stepped into our home. He surveyed the scene—Lisa
in handcuffs, me holding Laney close, Hekate clinging
to Meri, and Bonkers curled up protectively by her
feet.

"We're okay," I assured him, though my voice
trembled slightly with the aftershocks of fear and
magic. "Just shaken."

Jeremy nodded, his gaze lingering on Lisa before
turning back to me. "We'll take it from here." He
directed the deputies with a few short commands, and
they moved in to escort Lisa out.

Thorn came back inside just as they were leading her
away. He didn't say a word; he didn't need to. His
presence was enough to steady my racing heart. I
watched silently as they took Lisa into custody and
drove away into the night.

Once they were gone, Thorn scooped up the charm from where he'd left it on the porch. He held it out to me with a solemn look in his eyes. "Ready?"

I nodded. The girls watched with wide eyes as I took a deep breath and extended my hand toward the cursed object. A whisper of power coursed through me, warm and reassuring like an old friend's embrace.

With a flick of my wrist and a murmured incantation, I wrapped the charm in tendrils of magic. They glowed softly in the dim light before tightening like a vice. There was a brief resistance—a pushback from the dark magic within—and then it shattered into dust that disappeared into the night air.

A collective sigh of relief passed through us all—even Meri seemed to sit a little taller beside Hekate.

"I think," I began, my voice wry despite everything, "I may have been a tad overconfident about dealing with... well, with a normal." I met Thorn's gaze, and there was an unspoken understanding there—a recognition of my limits as a witch.

He stepped closer, wrapping an arm around me and pulling me against his side. "Kinsley," he said softly, "it's not about being overconfident. You're one hell of a witch—and you're human too."

I leaned into him, grateful for his warmth and steadiness. "Thanks for being there," I murmured against his chest.

Thorn kissed the top of my head gently. "Always," he assured me with quiet certainty.

The girls seemed to sense that the worst was over and gradually relaxed their grips on their feline protectors. Laney yawned widely—a clear sign that her adrenaline had worn off—and Hekate's eyelids drooped heavily despite her attempts to stay awake.

"Bedtime?" I suggested softly.

Laney nodded without protest, but Hekate managed a stubborn shake of her head before succumbing to another yawn that betrayed her weariness.

Thorn chuckled softly at our girls' antics as we began our nighttime routine—something so ordinary after an evening that was anything but. The cats followed us upstairs, Meri with his usual swagger and Bonkers ambling along behind us like he hadn't just been part of saving our family from despair.

As I tucked Laney into bed with Bonkers curled up at her feet like a vigilant guardian against nightmares, Thorn whispered reassurances to Hekate in her room across the hall.

Once we were sure they were both sound asleep—or as close to it as they could be after tonight's events—we retreated back downstairs.

The silence that enveloped us was comforting—a contrast to our earlier terror—and we sank onto our couch together.

"I know you're always there," I said after a moment, turning to look at Thorn in the dim light from our still-darkened porch light. "But sometimes I forget that even witches need saving."

He reached for my hand and squeezed it gently. "Everyone needs saving sometimes," he replied softly. "That doesn't make you any less powerful or capable."

Thank you for reading!

Made in United States
North Haven, CT
02 February 2024

48242698R00114